Being Different
is Okay!

Being Different is Okay

Acknowledgments and Dedication

I want to acknowledge those who played a major role in my development and support, both past and present, and who continue to make my life what it is today.

First and foremost is my mom, Dottie, who brought me into this world, raised me to be the person I am today and continues to support me throughout all of my endeavors, both as a mother and as a friend.

Of course, there is my dad, Bill, who always provided me with love, support and understanding. He taught me the true meaning of family and was the best father anyone could ask for. Though he has been taken from this physical world, his spirit is with me and I know he continues to watch over me and always will.

Also my children, Chad and Jillian, whom no one ever expected me to have, each loving me, always being there when I need them and teaching me that motherhood does not require an able body, but the ability to love and the desire to nurture.

I must not forget to mention their partners in life and the other parents to my grandchildren, Jenn and Josh, for they too support me; first, by loving my children, secondly, for caring for my grandbabies and thirdly, for always offering to help me when needed.

Most importantly, JR Hoirup, my husband, partner, best friend, lover and soulmate. He accepted me for who I am, supported me through the good and the bad, raised my children as his own and provided me with all of the love any woman/wife could ever expect or want. Were it not for him, I don't know if this second book of mine would have ever become a reality or my life be as fulfilled as it is and has been.

My friends, too numerous to name, know who they are and the role they have played in making my life what it is. I owe you so much and I love you all.

My acknowledgments wouldn't be complete if I didn't include the Northern California Publishers and Authors (NCPA), whose members encouraged, inspired, supported and provided me with the knowledge to follow through with my dream. Thank you one and all.

I dedicate this book to my grandchildren:

Michael Damien, grandma's first, who brings me joy with every smile, pride with every accomplishment and complete contentment every time I hear him say, "Grandma!"

Liam Jacob, grandma's second, even if it was only by two days, who has me wrapped around his little finger, smiles that warm my heart to my toes, filling my life with such joy just watching him grow and of course, making me whole each time he calls me "Grandma!"

Jeremiah William, Grandma's third, even if it was only by two days, who has such spirit and charm, is completely accepting of my differences, though he sees me so rarely and absolutely consumes my entire being with love, especially when I hear him squeal "Grandma!"

Lastly, there is Tobias (Toby) Glen, my fourth and at present, my youngest grandchild, fairly new to the family, melting my heart when he looks at me, as he toddles around so amazed at everything he encounters. I count my blessings every time I think of each of them.

Lest I forget, I also dedicate this book to any of my grandbabies who may come along in the future, for all are truly Laurie's Legacy!

Laurie Hoirup

Introduction

I hope if you are a young person reading this story, you will think about the life ahead of you and all that you are capable of with or without a disability. It is my sincere desire that you learn from this story that with love and support from family, friends and acquaintances, you can do great things. It may mean doing things differently from the norm, but the point is to do them and never give up.

I hope if you are a parent of a child with or without a disability, you will think about what you are teaching them about life; acceptance, determination, understanding and if nothing else, tolerance of differences in our world. Your children are what you make them and you have every opportunity to elevate their self-esteem and teach them to believe in themselves, as well as others.

I hope that principals, teachers, coaches, therapists, doctors, nurses, counselors and any other career specialists dealing with children will take away from this book that we can't always predict the outcome of any given situation, even when there are averages and patterns to go by. Instill in these young minds to go after their dreams, regardless of what life has handed them. None of us have a crystal ball and usually a positive attitude can be the strongest asset we have... So nurture those attitudes.

I have accomplished a great many things for someone with a significant disability. I climbed a tree, I went to slumber parties, I danced, I dated, I got married, I had children, I raised my children, I had grandchildren, I got sick, I survived, I got a job, I bought a car, I bought a house, I am loved, I am respected and my life has been worth living. Hanna is just beginning to learn the reality of that statement.

Of course, I owe all of this to my parents, my husband, my children, my friends, my colleagues, my extended family, my in-laws, my doctors, my dentists, my nurses, my teachers and everyone who has ever played a part in my life, regardless of how small. To all of you, I say thank you.

I want the story of Hanna to stand for something, to teach something, to enable young readers to understand we are all human beings with unique qualities and differences and yet, we all have similar needs, desires and goals. Being different is okay and once we all believe that, we will be better for it. As Hanna comes to realize, you need to like who you are!

Being Different is Okay

1. The Big Day Finally Arrives

Hanna's eyes popped wide open, though according to her bedside clock, the numbers read 5:00 a.m. She was thankful her mother had been so thoughtful, placing the clock high enough on the bedside table to allow Hanna the ability to check the time at any hour of the night. Of course, having her nightlight nearby and sleeping with her head slightly turned also made seeing the numbers possible.

Excitement was the cause of Hanna waking up so early, which always happened to her. She was starting her first day of school (no, not kindergarten or preschool), but actually going to attend her local grade school in person, something she had never done in her previous four year elementary school career.

Five years ago, Kindergarten had started out for her in a special education classroom in Crandall Lake, about 40 minutes from home. There was one teacher and two aides, along with 30 other students (none of whom she knew).

They ranged in ages from five to 13 years old and were in grades kindergarten through eighth. It turned out to be anything, but a typical classroom. The students worked at their own pace on individual projects, making it difficult to develop any form of connections, let alone friendships with peers.

Only one other child in the whole group was her age and was also in kindergarten. She turned out to be nice and all, but not someone Hanna could socialize with outside of school, especially since she lived about 40 minutes in the opposite direction. Actually, no one from the entire class lived near her.

It wasn't that Hanna didn't have friends; she did. Two of her neighbors were her best friends. Dana and Vanessa were sisters who got along well together, with Dana being one year older than Hanna and Vanessa one year younger. The three of them played together whenever they weren't in school.

Hanna's time attending Crandall Lake Elementary School proved to be short-lived. Her mother, Jesse drove Hanna 40 minutes one way to school, returned home and then went back to pick her up later in the day, making for two long round trips. Then Jesse learned that the only education Hanna was receiving had to do with play, which Jesse considered a complete waste of time.

For the entire four hours Hanna attended school, the aides played and colored with her and the other kindergartner. Not much teaching going on, resulting in limited learning. After all, Hanna already knew how to play and how to color.

Jesse became furious and rightly so! She could play with Hanna at home and didn't need to spend hours on the road to have someone else do so. She wanted her daughter to learn and thought that was happening in this Special Ed class. It didn't take her long, before she began expressing her dismay to the school board.

Jesse didn't always portray the calmest mother

when it came to her daughter's well-being. Some would call her a fighter and Hanna learned early on about advocacy, standing up for herself and fighting for her rights.

She planned to grow up to become an advocate herself someday and fight not only on her own behalf, but for others in similar situations with similar needs. She wanted to be the voice for those who couldn't speak up for themselves.

Mike, Hanna's father, behaved in a quieter fashion than Jesse. He was the more composed parent and usually the peacemaker. He was a big guy, strong and loving, and Hanna knew she could count on him. He always supported her mom, though he often became the voice of reason, if Jesse got too agitated with any given circumstance.

Not surprisingly, the school board met Jesse's demands. In no time at all, a tutor arrived. Mrs. Atkins was a teacher at MEADOWGREEN Elementary, which was a couple of blocks away from Hanna's house, where she tutored Hanna every day for two hours after the regular school day ended. Hanna no longer attended Crandall Lake Elementary.

This must have been a very long day for Mrs. Atkins, but she never appeared tired or agitated. She most often appeared cheerful and supportive, while making sure Hanna continuously learned something new.

Hanna's personalized program allowed for working at her own pace. By the end of her initial kindergarten year, she had already completed both kindergarten and first grade, putting her a year ahead of kids her same age.

Throughout the next few years, Hanna followed the same curriculum as her in-school classmates. Unlike several of them, she excelled, maintaining a straight-A report card.

Hanna loved Mrs. Atkins, loved learning and thought of school as fun. She also loved her mother dearly, but spending all day with mom and then several hours with Mrs. Atkins, didn't leave her much time, if any, to socialize with her neighborhood friends during the week. Hanna experienced quite a bit of upset and little happiness with her educational scenario.

She did visit school on holidays for the parties and also on picture day, so she would be included in the yearbook, but that summed up the extent of her attendance. She so enjoyed herself whenever she went and always hated having to go home. Every night she would pray that someday, she would be able to attend school just like everyone else.

Hanna continued her education like this through the fourth grade, with only one change in her routine. Mr. Gavin became her new tutor that year because Mrs. Atkins had retired. Otherwise, it was business as usual.

Mr. Gavin definitely appeared young compared to Mrs. Atkins, in several ways. Most obvious was that he had a full head of dark curly locks and she had thinning gray wisps of hair.

For Hanna, the most significant difference had to do with how he always acted funny, unlike Mrs. Atkins, who generally behaved quite seriously, though kindly. He certainly made learning fun, always using silly teaching methods, whereas Mrs. Atkins taught in a pretty traditional style.

He wondered why Hanna didn't go to school with the rest of her classmates, so one day he asked her and Jesse. He certainly saw no reason why she couldn't join the other children in school and frankly, disliked the whole tutor/stay at home thing.

Not that he disliked tutoring, but he believed strongly in mainstreaming; which coincided with his philosophy about teaching children with disabilities. He felt they should be included with their peers. Hanna knew nothing about his teaching ideas and only cared that he asked the question. She remained hopeful that he would help her to attend school like everyone else.

They had no specific answer to the question. Jesse just assumed the school wouldn't allow Hanna to be there without a Special Ed classroom or aide on hand and the subject never came up with Mrs. Atkins or the principal, Mr. Risner.

Hanna's young age kept her from asking such things, though she did long to go to school with her friends. They did have to face one valid concern standing as a barrier; Hanna's health. The winter months and cold weather posed a real threat to her life.

Hanna's disability resulted from a neuromuscular disease; spinal muscular atrophy (SMA 2) caused by an autosomal recessive gene, which sounds scary. In other words, she inherited it from both her mother and her father, leaving her with weakened muscles in all four limbs (her arms and her legs), and requiring the use of a wheelchair for her mobility or for someone to carry her from place to place.

Luckily, she was fairly small compared to other 9 year-old girls, in both height and weight (4'6" tall and 52 lbs. soaking wet), which made it possible for most everyone to assist her in getting around.

SMA has four different categories and the younger the symptoms present themselves, the more severe the effects. If the symptoms are seen in an infant, they don't usually live for more than a few years (SMA 1).

Thankfully, Hanna didn't start showing symptoms

of anything being wrong until almost her second birthday (SMA 2), which meant she would probably have a normal life span; living well into old-age (she hoped so).

SMA 3 symptoms appear in teenagers, who can continue walking well into their 30s and 40s. SMA 4 symptoms don't appear until much later in life and minimal weakness will occur. Hanna didn't get lucky enough to have either of those types, but at least, she didn't have Type I. She didn't feel that SMA 2 was scary at all.

The way SMA works is quite interesting; the brain sends a message to the spine, where there are motor output cells that act as outgoing messengers for all body movement and muscle activity.

The other cells located in the spinal cord are for sensory input and they carry messages of feeling/touch and temperature back to the brain. Of course, all of this happens spontaneously without any awareness from us.

Hanna had complete feeling throughout her body because her incoming messenger cells worked like they were supposed to, but her muscles were weak because the number of her motor output cells were limited and they didn't deliver the messages correctly.

When muscles don't get messages or stimulation from within, they atrophy, which means they die and go away. Hanna considered it important to understand that many parts of our body function because of our muscles, and our bodies are weaker than a young baby when our muscles don't work properly. It made her feel in charge of herself.

Most important to Hanna's well-being was her respiratory system; which is another name for our breathing mechanism. Hers didn't work as well as everyone else's, requiring Hanna to take a great deal of precautions, especially in the winter time, when it came to cold and flu season.

Her weakened muscles left her unable to cough, like most people and a cold could easily turn into pneumonia, which could ultimately kill her. Jesse and Mike responded by being extremely, protective of their daughter's health.

Luckily for Hanna, she had been raised in the same small town, with the same people, since before kindergarten, so most of the community knew her and her capabilities. They were also aware of the risks she faced day to day. They unconditionally accepted her; disability and all, doing whatever they could to keep her safe.

Hanna's friends knew all too well how dangerous it could be for Hanna to become ill with a cold. They had all been warned by Jesse, time and time again, to stay away from Hanna if they were ever sick and to be sure not to breathe on her and spread their germs. They understood the seriousness of the situation and promised to do their part to keep her healthy. They truly were a great group of friends.

Many of the town's youth had babysat for Hanna over the years and her neighborhood playmates also helped out with much of her care. They were all familiar with pushing her wheelchair, as well as assisting her with using the restroom.

Hanna's disability never posed a problem for anyone. Because she was small and lightweight, they could each continue to do their part. Hanna was so happy her parents had picked such a great place to buy their home to raise their little girl.

Because of this, everyone agreed Hanna could attend school with everyone else, beginning in fifth grade, except for the coldest months of the year; December-February, when Hanna was most susceptible to getting sick. During those months, the fifth-grade teacher (Hanna did not know who that would be), would tutor Hanna at home after school until spring came along, bringing in the warmer weather.

Several of her father's buddies got together and built her a custom desk for when she could attend school. For the desktop, they used a piece of plywood, about 3' x 5' and cut out a section in the center for her to pull up to in her wheelchair. There were four legs, each screwed in to a corner and making it the exact height she needed. It looked more like a table, except for the half circle cut out.

It took up the entire space behind the two rows of fifth graders in the classroom. The other two rows were the fourth graders, who shared the classroom in the small school.

MEADOWGREEN Elementary had only four classrooms; kindergarten had one to themselves, first, second and third grade shared the second classroom, fourth and fifth grades were in the third schoolroom and sixth, seventh and eighth grades occupied the fourth room.

The older grades had fewer children, whereas kindergarten made up the largest class of all, which is why they got a classroom all to themselves.

A gymnasium, which also served as a lunchroom, the Principal's office with a reception area, two storage rooms, two restrooms and a teacher's lounge, which supplemented as a small library, completed the rest of the school. This was a small school for a small community, but of course, to Hanna it appeared huge.

Hanna learned that Mr. Barton would be her new fifth-grade teacher. For all of her other needs, such as moving around school, having help with her books and lunch, and using the restroom, she would have to rely on carries the bride over the threshold. It is sometimes also referred to as a "Cradle Carry" because it's also how you carry a baby.

Hanna couldn't be carried in an upright position under her arms because it would hurt her back and neck, leaving her legs to just dangle and flop around below her. She also needed her head supported like a baby, as her neck muscles were too weak to hold it up herself.

Her legs were contracted at the knees because of sitting too many hours a day and not walking for a lot of years; they would no longer straighten out. Her knees were basically frozen into a bent position (a 90° angle).

This created another reason why she couldn't let them hang below her. They would surely get caught on something or accidentally get straightened out, which would literally break her leg.

There were many things she had to be careful about, more than most kids her age, but Hanna thought of it as just part of having a disability. She had no reason to complain, it was just part of her life.

Hanna's bed stood unusually high compared to all of her friends' beds. She actually had two box springs and one mattress; to keep her mother and father from having to bend over while dressing her and taking care of her.

It came from the idea of a hospital bed. This helped to prevent them from injuring their own backs, rendering them unable to do Hanna's care. That would be a real problem if Jesse or Mike couldn't take care of her.

Hanna felt like the princess in the "Princess and the Pea" story. All of her friends liked her bed a lot too. It was like being half way up to the top bunk in a set of bunk beds. Since she couldn't roll herself over, Hanna had no fear about falling out of bed from that high distance. She liked being way up off the floor; she felt safe.

In addition to her tall bed, she used a lightweight silky, nylon blanket, so the weight of the blanket didn't cause her legs to fall asleep. Anything heavy would impede (slow down) the blood flow to her legs, causing her legs to fall asleep and she would wake up in pain.

She had all kinds of little tricks, which helped her keep her life functional. Her special comforter wasn't only practical, but like her tall bed, it also made her feel like a Princess.

Hanna usually slept on her back for most of the night, but almost always started out on her left side with her hand hanging over the edge of the bed. She could still roll herself from her left side to her back, but was unable to roll from her back to either side or from her right side to her back.

Besides, sleeping on her right side caused her pain; she had a nerve under her rib cage, which would burn when laid upon for too long, so she avoided lying on that side altogether.

On her back, Hanna would keep her legs up close to her body, often supported by one of her hands. This way, she could move them away from her body a little bit when necessary and bring them back towards her to get more comfortable. These simple, small changes in her position enabled her to sleep for most of the night without waking up.

However, there were times when she still needed to call one of her parents to turn her because something on her body became uncomfortable or had fallen asleep. Her mother learned to do this in her sleep, almost like sleepwalking and she didn't remember doing so most mornings, which proved to be a good thing. At least, Jesse didn't feel as though her sleep got interrupted.

Considering Hanna didn't sleep very much due to

her excitement about her big day, she did not have to call Jesse once this night. She always liked those nights of not having to disturb her parents, but in this case, she hoped her lack of sleep would not leave her too tired herself for what lay ahead.

Well enough worrying about whether or not she was going to be tired. She needed to get back to the task at hand; getting dressed for her special day!

Hanna chose her pink A-line, cotton skirt, which hung slightly above the knees in length and a short sleeved, pink, green and white floral print, button up the front blouse with a Peter Pan collar, white mid-calf high socks and white patent leather flat slip-ons. She had personally chosen this outfit, which looked similar to one she had seen in the latest fashion magazine. She wanted to be modern and up-to-date with her wardrobe.

She would have her mom pull her hair back on either side with pink barrettes, accenting her just above the eyebrow length, cut bangs. She had polished her nails yesterday with light pink polish to match her outfit and her mom gave her a small dab of perfume. She felt quite grown-up and ladylike, with all of this coordinating of her fashion accessories.

Of course, getting dressed always began with her hard plastic body corset, which she had to wear every day to support her curved spine and help her breathe better.

Hanna had been afflicted with a scoliosis; a curvature of her spine, since the age of two because of her weakened muscles on one side of her body, which failed to hold her body up straight.

She originally wore a cloth corset, but by the time she was six years old, it no longer provided her with the necessary support and she had to start wearing a hard plastic brace (it looked like a bullet proof vest).

Wearing the brace didn't bother her, it fit her like a second skin, but what did bother her greatly had to do with the way she had to be fitted to create it.

She would wear nothing, but a skintight, undershirt material like tubing, from her shoulders to her knees; similar to a dress. Then a leather strap cupped her face and went around the back of her head with a hook at the top, which hung her from the ceiling.

She started out sitting on a stool, but slowly got hoisted into the air until her bottom lifted about an inch off the seat and her body dangled in midair in order to get her as straight as possible. It caused her quite a bit of pain, but at least her body wasn't all crunched up.

Once hanging from the ceiling, they wrapped her torso in a moist plaster of Paris (a gooey bandage like material when wet, hardening as it dries) until it measured about a quarter of an inch thick all the way around her. After being allowed to dry and harden, it got cut up the middle, including the undershirt fabric, which became its lining.

The whole process only took about 10 minutes, but long enough to cause her jaw to lock into place after supporting all of her weight, even for that short amount of time. To Hanna those 10 minutes seemed like an eternity.

Initially, she didn't experience any pain, but after about two or three minutes, tears began to involuntarily slide down her face. With every ticking second, the throbbing would increase and by the time they brought her down from that contraption, she felt like her head would surely explode!

It took her close to an hour before being able to open her mouth again, after locking in place and also for the pain to subside.

After the brace dried and they cut up the middle to

remove it, she was actually naked for a few minutes, but she didn't even think about it, nor did she ever feel embarrassed because all of her concentration focused on the intense pain she was experiencing in her jaw.

She wouldn't have cared if the whole world saw her at that moment in time, but luckily, only her mom and the orthotics technician (brace person) were there.

Hanna also had the pain of getting used to each new brace with sore spots on her rib bones and hipbones, but most of it subsided with time (about two weeks) and padding galore. Thankfully, she only had to go through this process about once every eight months, as her body was continuously growing and changing.

She looked forward to her figure developing and growing up, but oh how she dreaded this other aspect. She hoped and prayed that by adulthood, the time frame would be much longer between fittings because her body would be all done growing and all she had to worry about was if the brace wore out.

Now, with a cast of her body, the final steps included soaking it in a plastic coating, trimming the edges in leather and adding Velcro straps for opening and closing.

Her body corset became as much a part of her, as her wheelchair, probably more so, because she started wearing it a few years earlier than using her wheelchair and she wore it many more hours a day than she used her wheelchair.

She didn't know life without either one; one provided her with mobility and independence, while the other one provided her support for better breathing, thus better health. Sitting up straight helped her lungs to work more efficiently, compared to being squished all the time. She knew to be quite thankful for both.

Getting back to the morning; her mom began dressing her by putting her body brace on first, and then her panties (which were also pink, like her outfit).

Putting on her brace was a process. It involved rolling her to one side, stretching the body brace open and kind of rolling her back into it. A little pull here and a little shake there and everything fell into place. Then the straps would be tightened accordingly to keep it in place. No big deal, just an everyday occurrence.

Panties were much easier to put on her. It simply involved Jesse putting each of Hanna's legs through the openings and then lifting under her knees with one arm to get her bottom off the bed, while pulling them up over her hips with the other hand. Jesse could accomplish both in just a few minutes, though it might take others doing it without experience, a bit longer.

Hanna's skirt went on pretty much the same way as her panties, but instead of her legs going through separate holes, they went through the same one. Next came her socks and shoes, which went on the same way as everyone else's, but Jesse had to be especially careful not to twist her ankles or bend her toes. They easily sprained, since they had no real resistance or fight in the muscles like everyone else.

Usually, if someone presses hard against one of your body parts, your muscles push back or hold strong, but in Hanna's case, that didn't happen. Instead, her muscles and tendons would tear or sprain, leaving her in a great deal of pain.

Also, where most of us heal in a timely manner, it took Hanna twice as long, because she couldn't do anything to strengthen the hurt muscle. Again, one of many things Hanna's caregivers had to be cautious about.

This second part of getting dressed; panties, skirt,

socks and shoes only took another few minutes after the corset/brace. The rest of the dressing procedure; the third part, got finished with Hanna sitting in her wheelchair.

Jesse lifted Hanna the same way she did carrying her to and from the toilet. One arm over her shoulders and behind her neck, supporting her head and the other arm placed under her knees for the honeymoon/cradle carry.

Hanna knew someday she would probably grow too large for people to carry her where she needed to go. She heard about a device called a "Hoyer Lift," which uses a sling and a hydraulic arm to lift people with disabilities, who weigh more than their caregivers can manage. It has a manual pump and wheels, enabling people to be moved from one place to another.

It sure is amazing all the stuff that's out there to help someone like Hanna live more independently. Maybe someday they'll make a motorized one?

Sitting in her wheelchair, Hanna finished getting dressed. Putting on her undershirt and blouse always started with her left arm, because she couldn't lift it as high (due to contractures in her shoulders similar to her knees). Her right arm went in easier, as the second in line, better at extending into the tight material.

Exactly the opposite had to be done when she got undressed; she always had to start with the right arm when taking things off for the same reason; more flexibility.

Hanna could still button her own shirt and Jesse expected her to do so. Since her disease was slowly progressive, the day might come when she wouldn't be able to do much for herself, so her mom and dad remained pretty firm about her doing anything she could by herself.

Hanna had no problem with this rule, as a matter of

fact, she completely agreed with her parents and besides, she liked being independent and doing things for herself. It also made her feel more grown-up.

For now, she had enough strength in her hands and arms to brush her own teeth, but unable to reach above her head to comb her own hair. Her mom acquired that job. Her dad generally didn't do too well with this one.

Today, it was just a matter of brushing it out and putting in a barrette on either side of her head. Hanna liked her slightly, wavy locks. They looked pretty without doing anything special.

Hanna had soft, thick, dishwater blonde hair with a natural wave, which hung gently around her shoulders. Her bangs were thick as well. They were cut just above her eyebrows, which meant she had to get them trimmed every few weeks to keep them out of her eyes. She didn't mind though, because this hairstyle was popular.

She was a pretty little girl, or should I say young lady, with a somewhat angelic look about her. Of course, those who knew Hanna, also thought of her as a good girl, but by no means could she be considered an angel. Well, maybe daddy's little angel!

Other than eating breakfast and brushing her teeth, Hanna was ready to go and it only took about 20 minutes for dressing and grooming. Breakfast consisted of a bowl of cereal; Cheerios and a piece of toast with peanut butter; one of her favorites.

Another 20 minutes gone by to eat, 10 minutes to brush her teeth with Crest toothpaste (recommended by her dentist) and from start to finish, it hadn't quite been an hour (Jesse definitely had the process down); 7:50 a.m.-time to leave for school, which began sharply at 8:20 a.m.

Hanna couldn't take the bus and the school was a bit too far for walking, so her mom had to drive her. Jesse lifted Hanna into the front seat, using the usual honeymoon/cradle carry and seat belted her in.

She just recently started wearing her seatbelt because for a long time Jesse preferred using her arm to hold her back when she needed to stop fast. As she got bigger though, Jesse recognized the importance of the safety strap, knowing she couldn't hold back Hanna's weight during a sudden stop.

Once Hanna had been safely loaded into the car, Jesse folded and loaded her wheelchair into the trunk. This proved to be no easy task, since the wheelchair was heavy and awkward to lift.

Folding it wasn't too difficult; you only had to lift the foot pedals up, remove the seat cushion and then grab the seat at the front and back, pulling upward and the chair came together almost like a folding desk chair. Then it could fit, lying flat on its side in the trunk.

Jesse made a point to have a blanket beneath it and also covered it with another one to be sure to keep it clean. She didn't want Hanna sitting in a dirty seat.

Several of Hanna's neighborhood playmates (Dana, Vanessa & Paul) hitched a ride, as they didn't particularly like riding the bus. For that matter, nobody liked riding the bus; too many rules and not "cool." Another positive thing about Hanna attending school; more bonding time with her friends and a good way to be part of the "in" crowd right from the beginning of the day.

These particular playmates were actually her next-door neighbors and they were siblings. They had known one another since she was five years old; each family moving into their respective homes just weeks apart.

Vanessa was one year younger than Hanna and a grade behind in school, whereas Dana was one year older and a year ahead in school. Paul, the oldest of this group, being three years older than Hanna, but only two grades further up also had a disability.

Paul's disability involved something wrong with his leg muscles. They contracted behind his knees, which means they tightened up, causing him to walk on his toes. He wore high top tennis shoes to help stretch out the muscles, but it took years for that to happen.

He never let it slow him down, other than in school, because he did miss a year from whatever caused his problem. Hanna never inquired about the specifics… She accepted Paul as he was, like she wanted her friends to do with her.

Hanna and her mom, along with her three best friends arrived at school at 8:05, allowing time to unload and get to class. Since there were several steps to get into the school, Jesse unloaded Hanna's wheelchair first and took it just inside the door.

Then she came back for Hanna and carried her to her chair, getting her all situated and comfortable. She did not walk Hanna any further into school or to her new classroom, but rather allowed Hanna her independence and newfound freedom to be like the other kids.

From here on out, Hanna's wheelchair would remain at school during the week, locked in the teacher's lounge to save Jesse's back from the loading and unloading every day. One of Hanna's three friends would go in each morning and bring the chair to the door, where Jesse would carry her to, get her seated and then be on her way. All part of the going to school plan.

Jesse knew Hanna would make her way and do just fine without her at her side. Of course, on the inside she worried, but didn't show any of that to Hanna. She didn't raise Hanna to be a mama's girl, but rather an independent, risk-taking, stand on your own two feet (wheels) kind of girl. Hanna was finally just like everyone else!

Being Different is Okay

3. Meeting Her Expectations and Then Some

Hanna nervously pulled in behind the cutout of her new desk, which already housed her notebooks, pencil box and other important items. Soon her textbooks would also find their place, joining her other school supplies. She had already decided where each would sit, as she liked being organized.

Her desk seemed quite large compared to her classmates, but theirs opened up and stored items inside, out of sight. She didn't have that luxury, as she would not be strong enough to open a desktop. It also meant she would have to keep her desk clean, but that wouldn't be a problem for her.

Her other classmates found their seats, hoping to be allowed to sit where they chose, rather than having assigned seating. She knew all 12 of the fifth-graders and probably 10 of the 14 fourth-graders, so she felt quite at ease. The small, rural community, primarily made up of farming families, where pretty much everyone knew everyone to some degree made this possible.

The bell rang promptly at 8:20 and Mr. Barton went to the chalkboard and wrote his name and date in large letters. He just started at the school and though the students knew each other, he didn't know any of them and probably wasn't aware of their familiarity with one another.

He then walked to the other end of the board and made a list of each subject they would be covering throughout the day. He made a schedule for them and suggested they copy it into their notebooks, which Hanna had already started doing, even before his instruction.

Each day would include language arts, spelling and/or vocabulary, math, science, social studies and/or history, art and/or music, penmanship and physical education. Two 15 minute recesses and one 40 minute lunch hour would complete the busy school day, which would end at 3:00 p.m. on the dot.

The books were handed out and everyone wrote their names inside the front cover in pencil, of course. Hanna piled all of her books on one corner of her desk, leaving the front unobstructed to be able to see the board and have Mr. Barton see her. She liked being noticed.

On the other side of her desk, Hanna stored her other school supplies, along with her lunchbox. That left all of the middle in front of her, open for writing notes, completing workbook assignments, reading from open books and sometimes all three at once. All part of Hanna's organized personality.

The day progressed nicely, everyone being friendly and supportive to Hanna. She ate lunch in the gym with the rest of her class and during recess she was able to have one friend stay inside with her because she couldn't get down the stairs to go outside to play and the grassy, playground did not work well for a wheelchair.

Today, she chose her close friend Vanessa and tomorrow, she would select someone else. She wanted to spend time with all of her buddies.

Thankfully, MEADOWGREEN Elementary was

fairly new and all one level, so Hanna managed to get to all of the areas she needed to inside. The gym, where they sometimes had PE, depending on the weather, also doubled as their lunchroom during the first half of the lunch period and a play area for recess on snow days. It provided a wide open area, easy to roll on with plenty of space.

She had access to all of the classrooms, the restrooms, a small library, which seconded as the teacher's lounge, the front office and even the supply room. This was important for the days she became her classroom's supply monitor.

The school was nicely laid out for wheelchair access, except for the outside due to the steps. However, the back door only had one step, so if she needed to get out of the school, there was a way to do so. She preferred staying indoors though, as did, her many friends.

Due to the humidity in the spring and fall, along with the intense cold in the winter, remaining indoors was always welcomed. In addition to the comfortable temperatures, they liked the element of no direct supervision. When Hanna and her chosen friend for the day were inside, they felt more independent and grown-up, being left to take care of themselves. This privilege helped to strengthen Hanna's friendships.

As she expected, she didn't have to use the restroom, but the eighth grade girls were available if she needed them. The school provided a cot in the restroom, so if she did have to go to the bathroom, the girls could lie her down on the cot to get her pants down. This would work out quite well.

It also came in handy for any other students who were not feeling well; they could go lie down to rest if necessary, especially since there school had no nurse or medical office where the students could go when ill.

Hanna appreciated everyone's willingness to push her wherever she needed to go, because the gym sat quite a ways from their classroom, as did the restrooms. Hanna couldn't believe all of the helpers she had. She would never be in need or at a loss for someone to assist her, this she was sure of.

At lunchtime, she sat with all of her close friends and they shared their lunches like kids do. Hanna had a peanut butter and jelly sandwich, which her mom cut into quarters to make it easier for her to hold, along with potato chips, two chocolate chip cookies and a banana. Of course, she'd never to be able to finish all this food, so the swap began…

Susie had brownies and Debbie had left over pizza. Hanna traded one cookie for one brownie and half of her sandwich for a piece of pizza. She enjoyed her perfect lunch with her perfect companions. Life doesn't get much better, Hanna thought.

The day went by much too quickly and soon the bell rang, signaling the end of school. Hanna's friends, who were riding home with her, helped to push her to the front door. It was there her mother met them, carried her out to the car and then went back in and locked her wheelchair in the teacher's lounge.

Leaving her wheelchair at school during the week didn't present a problem for Hanna because she rarely used it at home, other than for a few chores. Matter-of-fact, it was quite bulky and didn't maneuver well through the hallways, doorways and over the carpeting.

Besides that, when she was at home, she sat on the same furniture as everyone else did. She had a spot on the couch with a small table, which sat in front of her to hold her drink, the remote control and other stuff. At dinner time, Hanna got carried to the dinner table chair and of course, at bedtime she slept in her own bed.

As for the outside activities, Hanna had a special chair she used. Her "Hogue Stroller," named after its creator, looked almost like a refrigerator dolly; narrow, tall back with lawn chair webbing, aluminum frame (making it lightweight) and two go-cart type tires on the back, requiring the chair to be tipped backwards for pushing and pulling. Hanna affectionately called this her stroller.

The chair designed by Mr. "Hogue" came about because he wanted a different way to transport his son who had a disability; one that didn't look quite so medical and more functional than a wheelchair. Having the weight pivoted on the rear axle made the chair less heavy to the individual doing the pushing. Not only did the chair look different from other wheelchairs, but being lightweight, easy to handle and able to be pushed by even a small child, really made it the ideal chair for play.

Hanna found this chair to work with all of her friends of similar age and older. They were all around the same height and therefore, could easily tilt the chair backwards, allowing them to push or pull, depending on the situation. In many cases, there would be one friend pushing from behind, holding onto the handlebar, with another friend pulling from the foot pedal end, putting less stress on each of them. This became especially important when meandering through the tall weeds to their favorite treehouse.

Hanna's stroller enabled her to go hiking, camping, navigate narrow paths, go to the beach and travel wherever her friends could walk. This unique wheelchair gave Hanna a lot of independence. Of course, the one drawback was that she could not maneuver herself, but even in her manual wheelchair, her strength did not allow her to do much of that either, so she didn't see it as any great loss.

Hanna felt pretty confident she would have a motorized wheelchair sometime in her near future, as she didn't have the ability to push herself around much, but it would be even heavier than the chair she now had and just as big and bulky. She figured it would also be used for school and would probably live there throughout the school year. They did not have a vehicle that could transport such a heavy, bulky thing and it didn't fold up, so she didn't give it much thought for now.

Jesse came back out to the car and asked Hanna how her day went. That was Hanna's cue to open the floodgates! She just couldn't stop talking about how incredible her day had been, how much fun she had, how all of the other students were so nice, how great all the teachers were, how helpful and supportive everyone had been, how much she learned, how perfect her desk worked out and she just went on and on.

Jesse just smiled and repeated over and over again, "Uh huh, how wonderful, I am so excited for you sweetheart!" Hanna didn't even stop to take a breath between school and home. Her friends however, didn't appear to be quite as excited as Hanna.

Of course, the other kids were used to having a first day at school and somewhat knew what to expect. They may have been excited, but next to Hanna, they didn't hold a candle. For her, school meant more independence and socialization, which the others probably took for granted. They also didn't really have an opportunity to share their stories because Hanna didn't pause long enough to let anyone else speak.

At home, Hanna went straight to doing her homework and finished before dinnertime. She had a desk and a chair in her room, which she used when her wheelchair remained at school. Hanna didn't have much of an appetite this evening, still being so excited about school and all.

She had already told her dad all about it when he came home from work and had even called her grandparents and her aunt to tell them of her wonderful, exciting news! She couldn't think of anyone else to call, didn't really want to watch TV, so instead, she just went to bed.

Hanna also decided to go to bed early because it would make tomorrow get here even quicker and she could get back to school. Once Jesse put her in bed, she laid there for a while and figured out what she would wear the next day, planned her lunch for tomorrow, said her prayers; thanking God profusely for letting her go to school and while drifting off into a contented sleep, her last thought included; "August 23,1965, has been a great day!" School turned out to be even better than her expectations and her happiness overflowed!

Being Different is Okay

4. More than Reading, Writing and Arithmetic

As the days wore on, Hanna's excitement began to settle down. Not that she didn't love school every single day, because she did, but she knew what to expect now and she had a routine. She had other everyday activities, like dinnertime, homework time and bedtime, but nothing brought her the joy and satisfaction like going to school, which became her favorite thing to do ever.

Her daily schedule of classes didn't change much unless there were guest speakers coming to present on a particular topic or perhaps her class went out on a field trip, but generally she could depend on the activities of each weekday and plan accordingly, which worked out well for her organized personality.

Her mom made it a point to always send something different for lunch to surprise her and she enjoyed the variation from the norm. She also had many friends to choose from to stay indoors with her during recess and the more friends she made, the more choices she had for companionship and food. It took almost 2 weeks before she hung out with the same person.

The two 15 minute recesses, along with the remainder of time after lunch gave Hanna a lot of opportunity to get to know her new classmates and cement her existing friendships with her closest peers. For now, only girls stayed in with Hanna during these three breaks because she just didn't have a lot of close friends who were boys. She hoped maybe someday she would.

Hanna wanted to be friends with boys, but it just wasn't very common at this age. However, something new began to occur for Hanna; her interest in boys, as more than just friends was taking shape, creating a whole new set of feelings within her. One young boy in particular caught her attention. She shared this information with only her closest of friends; Debbie, Marion, Dana and Vanessa (the latter two were sisters and her neighborhood buddies mentioned earlier).

Yes, Hanna was experiencing her first crush. The young David, older than her and in the seventh grade had her attention. She knew he would probably never return the feelings, but it didn't stop her from daydreaming about dating him and maybe someday, going steady.

One day, during a review for a math test (she already knew her math well), Hanna decided to write a note to David, sharing her feelings with him. She had never written a love letter and for her first, she thought she did a good job. Of course, she never intended to give it to him or have him see it, so she hid it in her math book, where she eventually forgot about it.

David had a younger brother who was actually pretty friendly with Hanna. Ricky would often horse around with her, teasing her in a playful way and he usually treated her like everyone else. She enjoyed that and considered it a true sign of friendship!

Matter of fact, it was a big deal for her classmates to push one of the boys into the girl's bathroom or vice versa almost daily and Ricky usually managed to push her into the boy's bathroom at least once a month. Hanna would squeal and close her eyes, while trying to hold back on her wheels, but she couldn't match Ricky's strength and determination. Thankfully, he always took her right back out, but the battle was fun.

Hanna hoped her friendship with Ricky would trickle up to his brother David and maybe she would start out being his friend too. To her dismay, things didn't go exactly as she wanted them to. She truly believed David didn't even know she existed, but how could he not? Perhaps in time they would finally connect?

Sometime later in the year, one of her classmates accidentally bumped into her desk and knocked some of her books down onto the floor. Of course, along with the crash of her books, came the letter to David spilling out of her math book for all the world to see. Naturally, she had put David's full name on the outside of it. How stupid could she be?

Hanna could not wheel her chair quick enough to get to the letter, nor were any of her good friends close at hand. Instead, Tommy, one of the younger, less mature fourth-graders grabbed it and before she could say a word, he ran the letter straight to David.

Hanna wanted to die. Devastated and horrified, she couldn't imagine how she would ever face David again. Now he would think of her as a stupid little girl and all chances of ever dating him would go right out the window. She felt so humiliated and just wanted to cry. She decided she would just have to stay away from David, as best she could.

Her friends tried to be supportive and promised to help her avoid him; like this might even be possible in such a small school, but she could pretend, lie to herself and hope her fantasy would play out. After a few days, it seemed as though she just might succeed in her plan. It had been several days, since her letter was hijacked and the world didn't end.

As a matter of fact, Ricky had not said a word to her and surely he would have mentioned something if he knew about her crush on his brother. She also hadn't run into David at all and Hanna began to think, "Maybe that stupid fourth-grader, Tommy just threw it away." She could dream couldn't she? Her dream quickly turned into a nightmare!

The next day, her friend Vanessa was giving her a push to the gym for lunch and as someone opened the door for them (it's hard to push a wheelchair and open the door at the same time), she looked up and there jumped David, sinking a basketball through the hoop. The end of the gym near the door was still used for recess play, while the far side served as the lunch area.

David looked at her, their eyes met and he smiled. Hanna was beside herself, heart pounding, sweaty palms, not knowing what she should do. She instinctively smiled back and Vanessa somehow knew to push faster, as they quickly hurried to their lunch table.

Well, Hanna hoped eye contact and shared smiles would be the first step to a long and wonderful romance, but sadly, it didn't work out that way. Instead, Ricky and David's family moved to another town about a month later, sometime in early December and she had no choice, but to get over him. It didn't make a good Christmas gift, but luckily, Hanna survived the whole ordeal, assured by her mother there would be many other crushes along her path of growing up, some even reciprocated.

A few weeks after David's move, winter roared in with the fierceness of a lion! It happened to coincide with the Christmas break, providing for the perfect time for Hanna's tutoring to resume. She was lucky to have continued attending school through the first few weeks of

December and hopefully, would only have to endure the homeschooling for a couple of months.

Mr. Barton replaced Mr. Gavin as her tutor, since he taught the fifth grade and because Mr. Gavin had moved to a different school in a bigger town. Mr. Barton came by her home every day after school, once it was back in session in early January, with several quick lessons and homework to boot.

None of it presented any difficulty, but she hated doing the work by herself and not experiencing what her friends were doing. Each evening she trudged through the chore of schoolwork, saddened by each assignment.

Lunchtime seemed especially lonely, having no one to trade desserts with. Not only didn't she have her special recess time with her buddies, but she didn't even have any playtime with them either. By the time her tutoring finished, dark settled in and it was dinner time, so no time with friends during the week.

On the weekends, there were a few opportunities for play, but sometimes not even then. She missed them all so much. It was awful!

Hanna started keeping a calendar, diligently marking off each passing day. The few holidays in January and February, like Lincoln's birthday and Washington's Birthday were quite helpful in making the time go by, because her neighborhood friends were also out of school and they were able to spend more time together just hanging out.

By the time those dates had come and gone, Hanna counted on only having less than one more month to endure until she could return to her favorite routine. She couldn't wait to end her misery.

Hanna had decided several months ago she had an interest in cheerleading and now she needed to keep busy in order to mend her broken heart over David's departure and to stop feeling depressed over missing school. She started doing some extra credit projects, as well as learning as much as she could about sports; all kinds of sports, but mostly basketball. There was a method to her madness.

Hanna wanted to be like her friends in other ways besides just going to school. She selected cheerleading as her next challenge. Since basketball season had begun in early November, about two months before her time of confinement when tutoring resumed, she attended every game she could and diligently worked on her mom to become the cheerleading coach.

She had thought this up prior to leaving school for the couple of months, but it took shape once she became stuck at home. She used the time for more than going to games, it gave her the time to put her cheerleading plan into action.

Though she couldn't actually be a cheerleader (she had never seen a cheerleader in a wheelchair; probably because of tryouts, jumping, dancing etc.), she could certainly be there to support her friends and her team.

Besides, all the girls just loved Hanna's mom and enjoyed having her around. Most of them could talk to her about anything and often did so before going to their own mothers. Sometimes the girls would send Hanna home with questions for Jesse because they knew she would get a straight answer. Hanna thanked God for giving her such cool parents.

Hanna and her mom had a truly wonderful relationship. They were so close and there wasn't anything Hanna couldn't talk to her about. A lot of her friends were jealous of their mother/daughter relationship and wished they had the same thing with their moms.

Hanna never felt embarrassed or afraid to talk to her mom about anything and she loved that about her.

For this reason, Hanna knew her friends would support the idea of having Jesse as their cheerleading coach. With her friends and her mom on board with this idea, she knew the school would go along with it. Though she might not be able to attend class because of the weather, going to a game one or two afternoons a week during the warmer time of the day, as well as a few practices, would definitely keep her in touch with everything.

Jesse instinctively knew what Hanna had in mind and of course, she went along with the program. As the cheerleading coach, Jesse and Hanna would have to stay involved with school, even before Hanna had her schedule to return. Hanna could be sneaky when she wanted to be, but rarely did she get away with anything with her mother not knowing what she was up to. Of course, Jesse had to admit, she knew where Hanna had learned her tactics and certainly couldn't blame her. As they say, "Fruit doesn't fall very far from the tree."

So, in no time at all, Jesse and Hanna were holding practices twice a week at their house and going to games two days a week (weather permitting), leaving only one weekday when Hanna did not get to see her friends. She also started helping to make up some of the cheers and routines and before long, the girls were including her in all of their plans. Hanna even had her own pair of pom-poms.

Those plans now involved slumber parties and many other outings. In order to spend the night at a slumber party or be able to go to an activity for several hours, someone would have to help Hanna use the restroom. As her friends in school became more familiar with her needs and her care, they started to assist her with those things. No longer just her neighborhood friends or the eighth-grade girls, but instead, most of her female classmates could now help her out.

Another thing concerning Hanna had to do with her needing to be turned through the night. She wasn't sure how willing her friends were going to be to wake up in the middle of the night and reposition her, but she soon learned like everything else, it didn't present a problem for any of them. As a matter of fact, most of them were similar to her mom and didn't even remember waking up to turn her. Too funny…

Though her mother still generally went on the majority of outings, as either a chaperone or a driver, Hanna did not have to depend on Jesse for everything in order to participate. Hanna now received invitations to birthday parties, the movies, roller skating parties and shopping. No young girl's life is ever complete without these activities and now her life was well on its way to being everything she imagined.

When Hanna showed up at a roller skating party, she often got the strangest looks. She knew people wondered why in the world a girl in a wheelchair would come to a roller skating rink, but it didn't take them long to figure it out. As Hanna also quickly learned, rarely does everyone roller skate at once. There is as much socializing going on at the snack bar or on the sidelines, as there is skating on the rink.

Hanna wouldn't trade all of that socializing for anything in the world, but even Hanna learned a valuable lesson. Things could be done differently, yet have a similar end result; at intermission, the owners of the roller rink were so impressed with her determination and courage, they allowed her to roll around out on the rink in her wheelchair, because no one would get in the way to get hurt. It was one of her favorite times!

She usually couldn't push herself around very easily, because of the weight of her wheelchair, but the skating rink was so slick and level that it didn't take much strength to get herself going and then she just had to steer.

For approximately 10 minutes, Hanna could cruise around the rink with her hair flowing behind her, be-bopping to the music playing, and laughing at the sparkling lights all around her. She loved the sensation and figured this is what the other kids must feel when they were skating.

This was one of the first extracurricular activities Hanna learned to participate in with some form of modification. Actually, recess and cheerleading were also activities in which she participated with some adjustment, but she didn't think about those in the same way. She soon realized, with some simple changes, she could do almost anything. Having a disability demanded creativity, at least if you wanted to do more than sit around all the time and Hanna definitely had her creative side.

Shopping, one of Hanna's all-time favorite pastimes, didn't take much change or modification to participate, but purchasing clothing required some ingenuity. Since many of her friends were of a similar size, she would use them as her model. They would try things on in the dressing room, where she would join them, so she could see how things fit them and then visualize how the items would fit her. Though her tastes were similar to that of her friends, they were each unique and for the most part, chose to buy something different than the others.

Earning money for shopping presented another challenge. Jesse knowing the importance of chores, both for learning responsibility, as well as for earning an allowance, had no problem finding weekly and daily tasks for Hanna to do. However, her chores, like her other activities, required some adjustments to enable her to complete them.

Hanna had to dust the living room and though it took an hour to push herself around in her wheelchair to do so, it became one of her weekly assignments on the weekends when her wheelchair came home. Her mom could've gotten it done in 10 minutes, but where was the lesson in that?

Hanna also had to scrub the bathroom sink once a week (her wheelchair made her just the right height), another task taking her much longer than if her mother had done it, but at least she was earning an allowance and would have money for shopping!

Her daily chore, along with homework, was doing the dinner dishes. Now mind you, Jesse had to do a lot of preparation for Hanna to accomplish this job. Hanna wasn't strong enough to lift the glassware or the pots and pans, so her mom washed those first and left the plastic stuff for her to do. Then she sat Hanna on a bar stool, bringing her to the right height of the kitchen sink and she would start her dishwashing routine. Hanna figured her mom intentionally used as much plastic as she could during the day.

Sometime during her dishwashing career, Hanna had a small mishap. The way Hanna did the dishes involved her leaning forward and balancing herself with her elbows resting on the edge of the counter. One evening, the edge of the sink was ever so slick with the suds from the dish soap, Hanna's elbow slipped, resulting in her landing face first in the sink full of water "SPLASH!"

Jesse and Mike, of course, were never far away

and this particular time, her dad was there lickety-split to lift Hanna up to breathe. Not surprisingly, her dishwashing days came to an abrupt halt. They were not going to take any chances of something tragic happening. Hanna was going to miss doing the dishes… NOT!

If Hanna had been smarter, she would've thought something up like this a long time ago. Not really, she knew her parents were quite scared over this one and she wouldn't ever pull that kind of trick on them. Thankfully, she continued to receive the same amount in her allowance, though she had no new chores added to replace dishwashing, at least not yet.

So halfway through the fifth grade, Hanna had managed to navigate school, shopping, cheerleading, sports, slumber parties, skating and her friendships blossomed. Going to school turned out to be everything Hanna had dreamt about, imagined, hoped for and ultimately enjoyed. She didn't think of herself as having a disability, but rather she was just like everyone else. What a great first half of the year!

Being Different is Okay

5. The Best Birthday Present Ever!

January and February were the longest months Hanna had ever experienced. She thought by marking off each day on the calendar and doing all of the sports and cheerleading stuff, things would go by more quickly, but boy oh boy, was she ever wrong! She liked the times when she could see her friends, but what she looked forward to most was her birthday; it occurred in the spring and she would be back in school!

On Valentine's Day, Mr. Barton brought her a bundle of cards from her classmates when he arrived for their regular tutoring session, but it just didn't compare to spending time with her friends in school. Hanna couldn't attend the class party because it was too cold outside. Even the heart-shaped, chocolate cupcakes with pink frosting, which her mom baked especially for her, didn't make the sadness go away. They would have been wonderful to share with her classmates.

She didn't understand why schools didn't have Valentine's Day off? She thought, "A holiday is a holiday, so why do some of them get celebrated with no school?" She would have to research this occurrence for the answer… What she did know is the more school holidays she celebrated, the more time she would have with her buddies and there just weren't enough of them.

The days slowly ticked away; eventually downtown March 1 arrived and going back to school would soon follow. It seemed like forever, but finally the snow melted, the trees were beginning to blossom and the temperatures were rising… Spring definitely filled the air and Hanna knew it! Hanna liked the fact that her birthday, March 14, usually signaled the new season. Even though, spring did not officially begin until March 20, in her eyes, six days early didn't make any difference.

As far as Hanna was concerned, her birthday, along with the beginning of spring with its warmer weather, represented the ideal day for her return to school. It would be the perfect birthday present. Her birthday actually fell on a Monday this year, making the day an excellent choice for returning to school. She circled Monday, March 14, on her calendar with a bright, red pen and turned the circle into a star with little lines shooting out all around!

She presented her idea to her mom, who then shared the concept with Mr. Barton. Together, her parents and teacher proposed the start date to the principal, Mr. Risner, who agreed with the plan. Hanna could hardly contain her excitement when given the news and all she kept thinking was "Happy Birthday to Me!"

It only took her about an hour and several phone calls before her close circle of friends became aware of her upcoming return. Though it was only March 1st and she still had twelve more days to go, not counting today or her birthday, Hanna already started planning her outfit for what would be her first day back, as well as her birthday. She had to look just perfect for her special day.

She knew her mother would pack her the perfect back-to-school lunch to celebrate her joyous return and she could only imagine what kind of birthday surprise Jesse would include. Her mind continued to race in all kinds of directions. She needed to settle down, taking each day, one at a time. She would keep up with marking off the days on her calendar, in hopes they would seem to go by more quickly.

The calendar, along with the final practices and last games of basketball season, would surely make the time buzz on by. To her dismay, not only did the days not go by faster, but they seemed to drag on slower than they did in January and February. It appeared as though time was standing still. She knew that was impossible, but now understood the meaning of the phrase "a watched pot never boils."

Sunday, March 13 finally arrived and her family kept busy all day shopping, running errands and doing some yard work. The weather turned out to be quite nice and spring was definitely here a bit early. Hanna got to spend some time with her neighbor girlfriends and together, they planned for the following morning.

Eventually, the day drew to a close and bedtime followed. The difficult part for Hanna was going to be getting to sleep. She went to bed early in hopes morning would get here sooner, but that couldn't happen if she did not fall asleep. She tried counting sheep, singing songs in her head and going through her weekly plans, but nothing worked… She was going to be awake all night! She had to quit losing sleep due to her excitement.

When Hanna opened her eyes, her bedside clock read 6:00 a.m. She last remembered seeing 10:30 p.m., so she obviously fell asleep and now, the time to start getting ready for school approached. It was also her birthday; making her officially 10 years old! Her excitement equaled what she felt on the first day of fifth-grade, but then it was more about **anticipation** of what things would be like and today, it had to do with **knowing** what things would be like. Hanna was a happy girl!

Jesse finally came in at 6:45, giving Hanna plenty of time to wake up and be more than ready to go. She sang "Happy Birthday" to her daughter and then gave her a kiss. She told Hanna they would celebrate her birthday over dinner and she would have to wait for her presents until then. As far as Hanna was concerned, going back to school made the perfect present, so she had no problem waiting until evening.

The getting up routine mirrored the other school mornings; Jesse first carried Hanna into the restroom, then back to her bed to put on her body corset, panties, skirt, socks and shoes and then into her wheelchair to finish dressing and grooming. The one difference about today had to do with the way Hanna was feeling… She felt like a princess!

Though the weather had been warming up, it was still chilly this early in the day. Hanna chose a plaid, pleated wool skirt; pink, gray and white, with a long sleeved, button up the front white sweater, pink mid-calf high socks and black patent leather flats for her day's ensemble.

She had taken great care during yesterday's shopping errands to find the right outfit for her special day, having saved much of her allowance over the past few months. Jesse helped her to choose her perfect clothes and Hanna was pleased with her selection. Jesse had pretty good taste in clothes and style, even for a mom.

She had Jesse braid her hair this morning with a pink bow tied at the end and her heavy bangs were a nice accent. Jesse always let Hanna decide what clothes to wear and how she wanted her hair fixed. It was another way of giving her some independence. Hanna looked in the mirror and giggled; she looked like a schoolteacher, but that was okay, she might grow up to be a schoolteacher someday; one of her many future ambitions.

Hanna didn't have much of an appetite this morning, which wasn't uncommon for her when she got excited. She knew the importance of having a good meal for breakfast to feed your brain and keep sharp for school, so she made herself eat a piece of toast with peanut butter. That would give her some good protein and carbohydrates; both good for energy and muscles.

Most kids don't think about the food they eat or what it does for them, but Hanna knew a lot about nutrition and how different types of food affect different parts of our bodies. In regards to Hanna's disability, protein was critical for keeping her muscles strong, for as long as possible and carbohydrates provided her with the energy to do as much for herself as she could.

She also knew sugar wasn't very good for your body at all, so she tried to avoid eating too many treats. Luckily for her, she never had a sweet tooth and just one bite of a candy bar usually satisfied any cravings she might have.

After breakfast, with Jesse's help, Hanna brushed her teeth, checked her backpack for all of her school necessities and put on her coat. The last thing she needed was to get a chill that would make her sick during her first week back at school. That would never do! Knock on wood, Hanna had not been sick, since sometime last year before the summer and not even in school then.

As soon as she finished zipping up her coat (she

was still able to accomplish that feat), Dana and Vanessa were knocking on the door. Their older brother Paul didn't come along this time because he chose to ride with a different friend. The girls liked it better without him. They were together again and life was good. Hanna thought to herself, "We are like The Three Musketeers!" Of course, her dad would tease her and say they were more like the "Three Stooges." He liked teasing her.

After all of the happy birthdays and giggles, everyone got loaded into the car, buckled in and ready to go. The drive to school didn't take long, but once there, Jesse had to take Hanna's wheelchair out of the trunk and back into school. While Hanna was out on tutoring leave, her wheelchair came home in case they needed it for anything else. From now until summer time, during the week it would call the teacher's lounge home, though it would still come home with them every weekend. Hanna needed it for her weekend chores, if for nothing else.

Once her wheelchair was in place, Jesse carried Hanna up the few stairs and got her situated and comfortable. The other girls crawled out of the car and joined Hanna on the front stoop behind the outer glass doors. Her mom kissed her goodbye, wished her one more "Happy Birthday," as well as a good day and went on her way.

No sooner had her mom walked out the door, when many of her friends, classmates and other school community folks huddled around, welcoming her back. She could not have hoped for a nicer reunion. She certainly loved MEADOWGREEN Elementary School. With all of the commotion going on, they had to hurry to their classrooms and beat the morning bell, so as not to be tardy. That would not be a good beginning for this perfect day.

As Vanessa pushed Hanna through the open door of her classroom, she could not believe what lay before her. Hanna almost fell out of her wheelchair due to this amazing surprise. She was already excited about the greeting she received at the front door and never expected this kind of celebration. She was truly blessed with some exceptional friends and the school staff were just as wonderful. Hanna had to fight back the tears.

Pink and white streamers hung throughout the room with different colored balloons hanging from the ceiling every few feet. Welcome back posters covered the walls; one created by every classroom and signed by each of those class' students. Obviously, this took a lot of planning and decoration time; someone came to school quite early to get this done or they gave up their Sunday just for her.

In addition to all of this, everyone started handing her birthday cards and in the middle of her desk, stood a beautiful birthday cake in the shape of a schoolhouse. It had white frosting with a red schoolhouse trimmed in black. Black icing was also used to write "Happy Birthday Hanna!"

Hanna knew that birthday cake did not make the ideal breakfast food, but what the heck… it was a special day and it surely wouldn't hurt this one time. Everyone gathered around and sang "Happy Birthday" to her and then they all enjoyed a piece of cake.

This turned out to be the best language arts class she had ever experienced. However, Mr. Burton didn't forget to give them homework; their assignment related to the mornings activities and they were to write an essay about their best birthday experience. This was going to be a piece of cake for her… She laughed at her choice of words…

The rest of her day proved to be just as fun, as the beginning. She enjoyed each of her classes, lunchtime was divine, though she did not trade desserts, as they all had birthday cake and the best part of course, spending time with friends again! She couldn't remember a better day in her young life and this one would be hard to beat, as one of her best.

Jesse showed up with several containers; she obviously knew about the party ahead of time. She brought the girls home with plenty of birthday cake to share with the neighbors. After saying goodbye to Dana and Vanessa, Hanna went into the house and completely forgot they were going to have a birthday celebration around dinner time.

Once through the door, she could smell her favorite dinner cooking in the oven. Her grandma and grandpa (her mom's parents) were there and they were all sitting around the decorated dining room table visiting. Hanna loved it when her grandparents came from the city and she wished it happened more often than once a month. She should be thankful though, because her dad's parents lived far away in Arizona and many of her friend's grandparents were no longer living.

After about an hour and a half, Jesse brought in the pork roast and dumplings and they had a feast! It made a good treat for her grandma to have someone else prepare the meal, since she usually cooked the very same dinner whenever Hanna visited them. Grandma always let her help make the dumplings, so there were often small ones as part of the meal, but not today and that was okay. Rather than having more cake for dessert, everyone settled for ice cream and then Hanna got to open more presents.

Her parents bought her a new record player;

Hanna was beginning to enjoy music and her grandparents gave her $20 to buy a couple of her favorite albums. Hanna looked forward to shopping with her friends searching for the latest and most popular music and having great fun doing so.

Her aunt Marge, who lived in the city near grandma and grandpa couldn't join them, but sent a card, which contained money-$20. Her Arizona grandparents also sent money, another $20. She felt quite wealthy. Hanna decided to save her $50 for something down the road and only spend $10 for new records. Hanna considered herself to be thrifty and liked to save money.

Her grandparents didn't stay late because of the long drive back to the city and it was a school night for her, a work night for her dad and it had been a long day for everyone. Hanna felt exhausted and still had some homework to do. She kissed them goodbye and Mike carried her to her desk in her room to complete her homework.

Hanna wrote and completed the favorite birthday essay in no time at all, because she had already thought about what to write throughout the day. Her other two assignments included making up sentences with her spelling words, which were easy for her and then she had 10 math problems to do. They were long division and she had no difficulty with long division either, so she completed her homework after about an hour.

By the time dinner and dessert were done, her grandparents gone and her homework complete, it was almost 8:00 p.m. She would typically watch some TV to wind down before her 9 o'clock bedtime, but tonight she had no need for relaxation time. Hanna headed straight for bed (with her mom's help, of course) and fell asleep before finishing her prayers. Her last thought before falling into a deep slumber went something like this, "Happy Birthday to Me and Thank You God for the best birthday present ever!"

6. Goodbye Fifth-Grade, Hello Summer Break

Hanna completed fifth-grade without a hitch. She never got sick, she maintained a 4.0 grade point average, she became part of the cheerleading squad, indirectly and she participated in all kinds of fun things with her friends; both her long-term buddies and her newly formed friendships. It had been a wonderful year!

On her final day of school, the bell rang for the last time of her fifth-grade year and though she excitedly anticipated sharing many summer adventures with her friends, she still had to hold back some tears, as she said her final goodbyes to some of those she would not see until fall and some not at all. It had been a really great year for Hanna and she knew the following years would just keep getting better.

She attended the graduation ceremony because many of the 8th grade girls had been her babysitters, as well as her helpers at school on the rare occasion when she needed to use the restroom. Hanna was very happy for each of them, but she would miss them and that made her a little bit sad. Thankfully, most of her friends, who were her age, could now assist her in the bathroom and she didn't have to rely on the older girls.

Summer vacation had all kinds of potential… Going to the lake to swim, going to summer camp and hanging out with friends, to name a few possibilities. There were actually two camps Hanna attended; MDA camp, a weeklong event for kids with some form of muscular dystrophy (SMA was included) and Peacock camp for kids with all types of disabilities, which lasted for three weeks.

Hanna would spend one whole month of her summer break at camp. It sure was a good thing summer break lasted three months because she had so many other things she wanted to do. First, she didn't want school to end and now, she needed more time for her summer vacation. It's funny how things turn out.

The summer started with a lot of free time and hanging out with her neighborhood friends. Some of the older kids had built a treehouse last year in one of the larger trees, a block or so behind their houses and now they were old enough to use it.

Her friends would usually pick her up in the morning after breakfast and using her stroller, they would push her down the path through the weeds and tall grass to get to their secret fort. Hanna always sat down below the tree, while the others were up in the treehouse, but they would take turns staying with her.

One morning, while they were making their way down the path, Paul suggested that Hanna should come up in the treehouse with them. Paul was 13, three years older than Hanna, and acted as their leader and protector. They all trusted him and got very excited hearing of his new plan.

There was a rope in the treehouse, which was fairly long and thick, so Paul believed it would be strong enough to pull Hanna and her stroller up into the fort. He figured if all three of them pulled from above, they could get her up there with no problem. Hanna, being the risk taker that Jesse raised her to be, had no problem agreeing to participate.

When they arrived under the big oak tree, Paul climbed the ladder to get to the top and quickly threw the rope down from above. He made his way back down in seconds and soon they had tied the rope to the top of Hanna's chair in some good knots. Then they each climbed their way up into the treehouse with Paul in the lead, holding the end of the rope.

When they all reached the top, they wrapped the rope around a big thick limb creating a crude pulley system, unbeknownst to them. Then the three of them, Paul age 13, Dana age 11 and Vanessa age 9 pulled with all their might. Within seconds, Hanna was being hoisted through the air fairly easily.

None of them had thought about this being dangerous, but instead, were just excited to be together in the treehouse. Hanna couldn't believe she was up there with her best friends and the fort was absolutely cool! Of course, this would have never worked if she were in her regular wheelchair, but having her stroller made it all possible.

After spending several hours fixing up the place and making plans for future summer trips down to the creek to go fishing and uptown to hang out with other friends, they realized it was getting late because of the grumbling of their tummies. It was definitely time to head for home and eat some lunch. Maybe next time they would bring a picnic lunch.

With the same expertise they used for pulling Hanna up into the treehouse, they managed to lower her down ever so slowly and just like that, Hanna landed firmly on the ground, waiting below for the rest of them to climb down. She bubbled with excitement over this new adventure and couldn't wait to get home to tell her mom.

They moseyed down the path, back through the tall grass and soon they were at their respective homes, munching down on the greatest lunch ever. For Hanna, just a peanut butter and jelly sandwich with some potato chips on the side made up her meal, but because she was so hungry, it tasted wonderful. She had also decided to wait to share her adventure with her mom, until she finished eating because she wasn't supposed to talk with her mouth full!

When she chewed her last bite, with a full stomach, she excitedly began to tell Jesse all about her tree climbing extravaganza. Jesse, horrified at the thought of her young daughter swinging by a rope several feet above the ground held by three kids from the top of a tree, did her best to not show her fear to Hanna.

Instead, she told Hanna how happy she was for her daughter's adventurous good time, but strongly suggested she not climb any more trees, as it might be dangerous for everyone concerned. She didn't want the neighborhood kids to hurt their backs or fall out of the treehouse.

Jesse's ability to not overreact, but appeal to Hanna's common sense proved to be the best way she could have handled this situation. Hanna accepted her mother's direction without much thought and could see her point, so didn't offer any resistance. As quickly as it had happened, the crisis (in Jesse's mind) ended. She felt confident there would be no more tree climbing for Hanna.

During their afternoon time at play, Hanna explained to her friends why she would not be climbing the tree again and they accepted her decision without question. They knew Hanna to be the best judge of what she could and could not do and they never pushed her,

Eventually, all of Hanna's cabin mates arrived and they got better acquainted, as they unpacked and put their things away.

Since many of the girls had been here before, they knew the routine... Pick a name for themselves and spend the week battling for points for best cabin. They earned points for having the cleanest cabin, the cleanest and most well behaved table in the dining room with points from each meal going to a different winner and there were other numerous contests going on throughout the week for which other awards could be earned. The prestige for being the best cabin overall was all that mattered!

This year, the girls all agreed to call themselves the "Crystal Lake Lovelies" and they were determined to win. Promptly, at 5:00 p.m. the music came across the camp wide loud speaker system and everyone headed for the flagpole. There they were given the guidelines for naming their cabin, rules for winning points and mess hall instructions. Hanna looked forward to a good meal, as all that unpacking made her hungry.

Hanna's cabin got lucky, as their table wasn't too far from the serving counter and they had a low number (four), which meant they would get to be one of the first in line to get their food. They had already identified their table runners (two of the counselors, who would pick up the food from the counter and bring it back to the table) and with such a low number, they were going to be eating much sooner than most.

They had a traditional first night of camp kind of meal; hamburgers and hotdogs (their choice), French fries and fresh fruit for dessert. To drink, they had Hanna's all-time favorite "bug juice," a different flavor of Kool-Aid for most evenings. Before eating, a selected table led the group in grace and song. There was a lot of singing at camp.

After a fair amount of time for eating, it was time to clean up, which meant gathering up everything and having the table runners return all of the dishes and stuff to the counter, returning with a few wet rags to scrub the tables. Soon you couldn't even tell anyone had been eating at all. Then you were scored and dismissed according to how quickly and well done your table got cleaned.

The first night of camp always began with a campfire and s'mores. First, everyone gathered at the flagpole again, this time for the flag lowering ceremony. Then they headed to their cabins to change into warm clothes (the evenings were often chilly). Soon all the campers and counselors were sitting around the campfire, singing songs, stuffing their faces with s'mores and getting the schedules for the week ahead.

Hanna returned back to her cabin by around nine o'clock and she was more than ready for bed. It had been a very long and exhausting day. Nancy had her undressed, in her pajamas, teeth brushed and in bed by 9:30. Lights out occurred at 10 PM, so Nancy had plenty of time to shower and get herself into bed.

At 9:45, the medical staff did their rounds, just to be sure everyone felt okay and weren't having any problems. Hanna was ever so grateful when the lights out song came over the loud speaker and probably fell asleep within five minutes, thereafter.

Each day had a routine and yet, something different going on, as well. They all got up at the same time every morning, had breakfast at the same time, though thankfully, the food changed every day. Hanna especially liked French toast mornings. After breakfast they would have their flag raising ceremony and then each cabin would return to clean up before going to their assigned activities for the morning. During their time away, the cabins were inspected and points allotted.

The schedule included an hour of archery or riflery, which alternated each day and an hour of arts and crafts or sports, also alternating and they occurred before lunch. Then after eating, there was an hour of rest. During this time, Hanna would usually write a postcard to her mom and dad or grandparents and when she wasn't writing, she spent her quiet time reading one of her favorite books; one of the Nancy Drew mysteries. This time became especially important to Hanna, just to rest her body and gear up for the afternoon schedule.

When they heard the music, it signaled the time to go to their assigned afternoon activities. They would participate in an hour of canoeing or fishing and an hour of swimming or horseback riding, which also alternated daily, just like the morning events. Of course, each cabin had a different schedule with two or three cabins at each activity. Hanna was happy to have swimming in the afternoon, when she knew it would be nice and warm. She enjoyed most of the activities, though she considered sports to be her least favorite.

Hanna didn't much like having to adhere to a schedule, but she realized with so many campers, things had to be organized. Thankfully, every time the camp loudspeaker started playing music, whether for waking up, meeting at the flagpole, going to a meal, beginning and ending each activity or lights out, the music always came from the most popular radio station, which Hanna enjoyed.

Though, the days were fairly routine, the evening goings-on were always different. The first and last night of camp was a traditional campfire, but the nights in between ranged from Carnival night, casino night, talent show, a dance and a movie night. Each event made for a lot of fun. There was also a weeklong scavenger hunt going on.

This particular summer, Hanna learned how to roll over and float on her back. The swimming staff thought it would be a good idea for her, since she couldn't lift her head out of the water. This way, if she were to ever fall in, she could roll herself over onto her back and then float for however long it was necessary, until someone came to her rescue.

Of course, she had no guarantee, even with her new found ability, that she wouldn't drown, but at least, she had a chance now. Hanna even won first-place in the floating contest for staying afloat the longest. She couldn't wait to show her mom and dad her new skill.

They had another traditional hamburger/hotdog meal for their final dinner and during this time they learned about their points and the winner for this week's all around best cabin. Sadly, the Crystal Lake Lovelies did not win, but they managed to come in second place, which isn't so bad. They always had next year…

The last night's campfire always ended up being sad with the many goodbyes… Hanna wished she could see all of her friends year-round, but most of them lived too far apart with camp situated somewhere even further away. Besides, she would only be home for a few days before going on her next camping adventure.

The last day arrived and there were lots of tears on the bus ride home. Once they pulled into the bus terminal in Chicago, tears dried up and smiles appeared on everyone's faces, as they greeted their families. Beautiful memories would have to hold Hanna until next summer. Hopefully, Nancy would return and be her counselor for another year.

Hanna's time home allowed for Jesse to do her laundry and get her packed again, while Hanna got to spend a few hours visiting with her neighborhood pals. Soon she headed back to camp; Peacock Camp this time, only a short distance from her hometown. Though she would only be a half an hour or so away this time, she would be gone for three whole weeks. That's a very long time to be away from your family and friends.

For the most part, the activities at Peacock Camp were similar to those at MDA camp, both day and night, but they swam in a pool, instead of a lake and they had a family barbecue about halfway through the camp session for families to come visit. Also, instead of having one counselor per camper, they had one counselor per room (they were like in a dorm, versus a cabin) with five campers in each. The counselors were older too, in their early 20s, compared to mid-to-late teens.

Another major difference was that each of the campers had a different type of disability, not just SMA like Hanna and they didn't need as much help. Since not all the kids needed physical care, they could have one counselor per room.

This year, one of the girls in her cabin had spina bifida, which is a disease where the spinal cord doesn't close properly and she had no feeling from her waist down, but she could walk on crutches and take care of herself. Jeannie and Hanna knew each other from last year. They got along well and were good friends.

Another girl had a mild case of cerebral palsy, which is a type of brain damage. She could still think and everything, but she walked kind of funny with a gait, which means she limped and her knees kind of crossed. She also had a speech impairment and had to talk slowly in order to be understood. Linda was very nice.

Kathy the fourth roommate was blind, but very independent. She could do everything for herself and used a white cane with a red tip to walk around. Hanna was amazed at how well she could get around and do everything without being able to see. Her clothes were marked with tags and the markings were raised dots. It's called braille and it's like a secret code that Kathy could feel and then know what outfit and what color she had. Someday, Hanna wanted to learn braille.

Mary, her fifth roommate, couldn't hear anything and had been deaf her whole life. She could communicate with Jessica, their counselor, who knew sign language, which is a way to talk with your hands. Only Hanna required full personal care, but the other girls needed different kinds of assistance. They all did their best to help one another out, whenever possible.

As with her other camp, Hanna developed some close friendships. She knew Jeannie from the year before, but this year she got close to Mary. Mary taught her how to finger spell, which is the alphabet with your hands. In sign language, there are different movements you make with your hands for whole words, but it's important to know the alphabet signs, in case you have to spell something out.

Hanna learned the alphabet quickly, as well as some important signs like "bathroom." Learning the alphabet was easy since there are only 26 letters, but learning words proved to be much harder because there are so many of them. Hanna hoped to continue to learn more words over time, just like her speech.

The three weeks passed by much too quickly and once again, Hanna became upset about having to leave her friends and her counselor. She hated goodbyes and knew next summer was a long time away. After lots of hugs and tears, Hanna's parents arrived to take her home. Even though seeing them made her happy, her heart was breaking.

However, her sadness quickly disappeared with thoughts of her neighborhood friends and the upcoming school year; after all, she would be a sixth-grader with lots of school experience. Her mom always said that when one door closes, another one opens and she was just beginning to understand what Jesse meant.

The summer ended with one final trip to the lake over Labor Day weekend. Hanna's family went with several other families and they had a big barbecue. School started the next day, but thankfully, the barbecue helped to keep Hanna's mind off of her first day as a sixth-grader.

Everyone was swimming, playing and having a wonderful time. Hanna balanced herself sitting on the edge of the pier, out of her stroller, dangling her feet in the water. Jesse stood about thigh deep in the water, next to Hanna with her arm draped loosely around Hanna's waist, looking back and talking to a friend. Hanna decided to show her mom what she had learned at camp.

Without any warning, Hanna threw herself forward into the lake and before Jesse could make a move to reach her, Hanna had rolled over onto her back bobbing up and down on the small waves of the water, grinning from ear to ear; "Look mom, see what they taught me to do at camp, so I don't drown if I fall in!"

Jessie, in her typical, composed manner, though her face had turned as white as a ghost, replied, "That's wonderful sweetheart, I'm so proud of you!" Of course, deep inside, Jesse wanted to drown her for scaring her half to death!

By the time they got home, the lateness of the hour made everyone tired, so Jesse helped Hanna head right for bed. Hanna didn't even take the time to plan her outfit beforehand, which she usually did before getting into bed. She did however, take a half an hour or so in her mind picking out her clothes for the following day. After all, she was a pro at this school stuff and didn't need to worry like she did the year before. Hanna slept well, dreaming about all the wonderful things that were yet to come.

8. Nothing Like She Imagined

Hanna may have tried to convince herself that she didn't feel nervous about beginning the sixth grade, but waking up an hour before her alarm was set to go off, clearly indicated the opposite! Though she had laid awake the night before planning what she was going to wear, she had now changed her mind at least three times.

As Jesse came through her door, Hanna immediately began talking... First about her clothes, then her hair and last but not least, her lunch. Of course, Jesse experienced no surprise at all by her daughter's morning enthusiasm. She had grown to expect this kind of behavior from Hanna whenever something new and exciting happened.

The morning routine began like all others; first, Jesse carried Hanna into the bathroom in her typical honeymoon carry, where she quickly relieved herself, followed by Jesse cleaning her up. Then they went back to the bed to start dressing. Her body corset and panties didn't take any thinking on Hanna's part and Jesse just proceeded through the motions.

Hanna picked out her red, white and blue print

culottes, the ones she wore for the Fourth of July. She wasn't worried about anyone remembering them because she wore a different shirt. It was a short sleeved, bright red, button up the front blouse, accented by her white anklet socks and white patent leather flats.

Jesse had her up and dressed in no time, pulling the sides of her hair back into a white barrette across the crown of her head. The rest she let hang down around her shoulders. She still had bangs, though she was thinking about letting them grow out. Fixing her hair like this kept it out of her face, which worked well for her because Hanna couldn't push the hair back out of her eyes on her own, but she was looking for a more grown-up style.

Hanna scarfed down her bowl of Rice Krispies and a glass of orange juice. Then Jesse pushed her back to the bathroom for Hanna to brush her teeth. She smiled into the mirror, making sure she had nothing stuck on her teeth or around her lips. When she felt satisfied that everything looked as it should, she was ready to leave for school.

Her wheelchair would be moving back to school, except for the weekends, which meant she would be sitting on her chair at her vanity/desk in her room to finish getting dressed each morning. When her wheelchair remained at school, she brushed her teeth at the kitchen table using a bowl and a cup. Jesse found her a small mirror to sit on the table. She liked being able to watch what she was doing. Her mom thought of everything.

Just as Jesse carried Hanna out to the car, Dana and Vanessa dashed across their yard to catch a ride with them. There was never any question about them coming along, they were of course, best friends and did many things together. Sharing a ride just made sense. Besides, it gave them a chance to catch up on things before starting their day at school.

Within moments, they settled in their seat, belted in and Hanna's wheelchair was placed in the trunk. It laid on a quilt, which had become the "wheelchair pad" and was covered with another blanket called the "wheelchair cover." Taking the time to pack her chair gave the girls more visiting time, which they always appreciated.

Ten minutes later, they arrived at school. It was only 8:00 a.m., but Hanna much preferred being early, having time to get situated and visit a little bit before the bell rang. It took a few minutes to get her wheelchair unloaded and into school, along with a couple of minutes for Jesse to carry Hanna to her chair and get her comfortable. After a quick goodbye, the girls were on their way to their new classroom. Hanna could sense all of the excitement in the air.

This year, Hanna would be sharing a classroom with the seventh and eighth graders. Just like that, she dropped to the low man on the totem pole, unlike last year, when she shared a room with the fourth-graders and enjoyed the role of one of the top dogs (she had heard that from her dad). Hanna could accept not having seniority because at least now, she was classified as being in the upper grades and an upperclassmen. That held its own kind of superiority.

It was however, going to seem strange not having Vanessa in her classroom like last year, but now Hanna would be in the same room as Dana and Paul. Since recess and lunch were different for the upper grades, Hanna would not see much of Vanessa during the school day, which kind of made her feel bad. They would have to make up for it by spending time together after school and on weekends.

Hanna's desk had already been moved to the new

classroom and set up by her dad over the weekend. Just like in her previous classroom, where she sat right behind the fifth-graders, her desk taking up the back of both rows, she again, sat directly behind the two rows of sixth-graders. Within minutes, she unloaded her backpack and put all of her new school supplies into their assigned space. Hanna liked her set up and left room for her books, which would be handed out at the beginning of class.

Each of her subjects were pretty much the same, except more difficult than the ones the year before. That didn't worry her at all. She liked learning new things and she especially enjoyed a challenge. They were arranged a little differently with more time going by before recess. Each of her morning classes lasted 15 minutes longer than before, so the upper grades recess time occurred separately from the lower grades.

All of her subject classes happened before lunch, whereas afterwards, she had art or music and then PE before her final recess, which came right at the end of the day. She kind of liked it this way, because Hanna tended to be more alert in the mornings and started to fizzle by afternoon.

Art and music were relaxing and then during PE, she just kept score or did some of her homework, depending on the happenings of the class each day. She knew that just like last year; during recess she would stay indoors and one of her friends would be allowed to stay with her. She was thankful for that, as it would be lonely sitting in here all by herself. Sometimes, she sat by the back door and all the kids would come to see her.

Her teacher this year was Mr. Wilson. Hanna didn't get to know him well last year, but all of her friends said he was nice, giving her one more thing to be happy about. She certainly didn't want a mean teacher. Hopefully, he wouldn't give them too much homework, Hanna didn't mind homework, but she was quickly following the lead of her friends and much preferred longer playtime and more TV time, opposed to hours of homework.

As the secondhand on the clock ticked forward, several of her classmates began to walk through the door. For the most part, they were all familiar faces. Of course, some of the older kids she recognized, but didn't know them as good as the students who were in her class last year. Then she saw someone completely different! She was excited about this because she would no longer be the new kid in school.

Susie came walking in with a girl Hanna had never seen before. This new girl looked at Hanna and then, whispered something into Susie's ear and giggled. Susie got a funny look on her face, but quickly brought the girl over to meet her. She introduced Hanna to Kathy. Kathy had moved to town a couple of weeks ago, while Hanna was away at camp. She hadn't heard anything about this most recent resident. She liked the idea of having another good friend and she welcomed Kathy to their school.

Kathy didn't appear quite as friendly as the other girls. Hanna thought, "She acted nice and all, but just didn't seem to want to talk to Hanna, like her other friends did." Hanna figured it had to do with being the new kid.

She looked pretty and nice with fashionable clothes and the latest haircut. The boys were certainly charmed by her style, each one of them trying to sit by her and make conversation. Hanna not too sure about the whole thing, certainly wasn't impressed at all.

Soon the bell rang and everyone grabbed the seat they hoped to be assigned. Mr. Wilson introduced himself to the class, writing his name on the board, "Like we were going to forget our teacher's name," thought Hanna. She felt somewhat irritated with the way the morning had gone and her attitude clearly showed her annoyance. Before moving on, he quickly rearranged everyone's seating positions, much to their dismay. There wasn't much he could do to relocate Hanna and that made her happy, helping to improve her mood.

As the morning progressed, first through math and then science, Hanna forgot about the unpleasant start of her day. Soon she was practicing her best cursive handwriting and then the recess bell rang. She had asked Dana to stay with her, which she happily, agreed to do.

They walked down the hall with the other kids, but everyone clamored around Kathy. They all wanted to get to know her better. Hanna and Dana were in the back of the group and never got quite close enough to socialize. Maybe Hanna would have a chance during lunch. After everyone went outdoors, they returned to the classroom and just visited, never bringing up the topic of the new girl.

Soon everyone came back from recess, found their seats and were learning some new vocabulary words, which were also this week's spelling words. It made for an easy transition into language arts, which now they called English. Hanna couldn't figure out why the new title; they already knew English and this class mostly had to do with writing and grammar. She guessed it was because that's what they called it in high school.

After writing an essay about what she thought sixth-grade would teach her, she was learning about history; all about America, the pilgrims and the Indians. She did not particularly like social studies and welcomed the lunch hour bell.

Everyone quickly scrambled to the gymnasium/lunchroom and as before, many of them traded parts of their lunch, while other kids went straight to recess, not eating at all. Hanna could never do that because when she didn't eat, she got weak and would never make it through the afternoon.

Most of Hanna's friends from last year sat at her table and Kathy joined them, as well. However, she did most of the talking and everyone focused quite intently on her every word. Hanna tried to talk with her and ask her questions, but somehow she never got very far. With everyone chattering at once, Hanna couldn't carry her voice over the lunch time noise. So she just sat quietly and ate what her mom had packed for her. She never even got around to trading with any of her buddies.

In no time at all the bell rang, indicating it was time to return to the classroom. All of them hurried along, while Dana and Hanna kind of hung back from the crowd. Dana seemed to instinctively know that Hanna was not in the best of moods. She positioned Hanna's wheelchair in its correct space behind her desk and went to her own seat. All the while, Hanna tried to figure out why this new girl didn't seem to like her. After all, they hadn't even talked.

Hanna, grateful that her next class was music, knew it wouldn't take a whole lot of concentration. The music teacher, Mrs. Jones, an older lady with white hair, kind of round in shape, being quite short, reminded her of her grandma. She brought several instruments into the room and proceeded to describe what they were and demonstrated how each of them sounded.

To be honest, Hanna wasn't much into musical instruments or music in general and was lost in her own thoughts about how the day had gone. Thankfully, Mrs. Jones never called on her to answer any questions or ask her to try one out.

After music, they went to PE with Mr. Wilson (they didn't have a special PE teacher), and since her classmates had not yet started playing any games or organizing their teams, the day ended with mostly exercise.

Obviously, Hanna could not participate with this activity, so she could choose to just watch or go to the library and read. Usually, she would have stayed to watch her friends, but today, she decided to go read a library book and be by herself. She was feeling very sad.

PE ended and transitioned right into recess. Dana came and picked Hanna up from the library and they returned to the classroom to hang out. Dana questioned Hanna about what was bothering her, to which she replied, "Nothing really, I'm just tired from all the excitement of the first day of school." Dana had no reason to doubt her explanation and went on to talk about other things. Soon the bell rang and her classmates were filing in; laughing and talking to one another, but mostly to Kathy.

Hanna's schedule this year was a little odd, but she liked it. With all of her regular classes in the morning, her afternoon seemed almost like playtime... Lunch, music/art, PE, recess and then wrap up time. Hanna quickly packed up her things in her backpack, with nothing to take home, as Mr. Wilson didn't give them any homework on this first day. She figured they would get swamped in the next few days. Finally, the last bell rang and everyone headed out the door.

Vanessa caught up with Dana and Hanna right outside their classroom door and they walked together, this time with Dana pushing Hanna down the hall to the front door. Jesse had already parked out front waiting for them. She came up the steps, gave Hanna a big hug and asked, "How was your first day of sixth-grade?" Hanna smiled and replied solemnly, "Okay, I guess." Jesse had a puzzled look on her face, wondering what had gone wrong. She knew Hanna too well and her quietness was not a good sign.

Jesse picked Hanna up out of her chair and carried her down to the car. After getting her settled in with her seatbelt on, Jesse returned to the entryway, took Hanna's wheelchair to the lounge and returned in a jiffy, all the while wondering what had gone on at school to keep Hanna so quiet.

The girls had crawled into the backseat and were buckled in, as well. The rode home with everyone uncomfortably quiet… Even Dana and Vanessa were at a loss for words. When they pulled into the driveway, the girls jumped out and ran to their house, as they hollered back, "We'll see you in the morning."

Jesse took Hanna into the house and sat her in her favorite place on the couch. Then she sat down next to her and said, "Okay Hanna, tell me why you are so gloomy? What happened to make you so sad?" Within seconds, Hanna started to cry and told Jesse all about the new girl who didn't like her. Jesse held her and gave her the time to get it all out.

When Hanna finished telling her tale of woe, Jesse wiped her tears and suggested it might be her overactive imagination. She also pointed out that Hanna wasn't used to somebody else getting a lot of attention because last year, she had the role of the new girl, but now the time had come for somebody else to have a turn and Hanna needed to be understanding and less sensitive. Jesse assured her that within a few weeks, everyone would be friends and the newness of Kathy would wear off.

Hanna accepted Jesse's explanation and had a quiet evening with her mom and dad watching some TV. Truth be told, it had been a long day and Hanna was extremely tired, so she had Jesse put her to bed early, pushing all thoughts of Kathy out of her mind. She said her prayers and decided that tomorrow would be a much better day. She just needed to not be so sensitive.

Hanna fell right to sleep and dreamt about all the good times she had at school. She feared she would have nightmares about her terrible day, but surprisingly, she had good dreams about everything that usually made her happy at school. When she woke up, she felt much better and was sure that sixth-grade would be everything she had imagined it would be.

9. Bullies Burst Her Bubble

Sadly, Jesse could not have been more wrong. As the days went by, things did not get better. They actually got progressively worse. Kathy became best friends with many of Hanna's classmates and soon they were ignoring her. They would walk away from her when they saw her coming, they would whisper to each other, then giggle and pretty soon Hanna only had a few girls who wanted to stay in with her during recess. Even her lunch table wasn't very crowded.

Hanna started to dislike going to school. Instead of waking up excited and ready to face the day, she would wake up in a bad mood from having a bad dream the night before and her attitude was anything, but good. Hanna was grateful to have Dana always at her side. However, Susie, Marion, Debbie and so many others barely talked to her now. She seriously thought about going back to tutoring much earlier than December.

Not only did the girls avoid her at school, but she wasn't included in any of their other activities either. She didn't get one invitation to a slumber party or a roller skating party and that made her feel awful. Shopping was limited to Dana and Vanessa, but truth be told, Vanessa had made new friends in her class, since Hanna didn't see her very much during the school week and Dana had friends of her own from the year before.

Hanna spent a great deal of time reading and she almost welcomed homework, just to give her something to do. She didn't much care about what Jesse packed for her lunch, because she didn't have anyone to trade with. Sometimes, Hanna even decided to stay by herself during recess, just to give Dana and Marge a chance to go play (they were the only two friends she eventually, had left to ask).

She hoped that Jesse would come to her defense and straighten Kathy out, but she insisted that Hanna had to learn to fight her own battles and come to deal with this problem in her own way. Jesse also demanded that Hanna stand on her own 2 feet, which didn't make any sense, since Hanna couldn't stand at all. Hanna did not understand her mom one bit.

So the school year continued and things did not get better. As far as Hanna was concerned, they were the worst! One day during recess, some of the girls led by Kathy, came in to use the restroom. All of a sudden, they started walking like Frankenstein or some kind of robot and they began chanting, "Robots in a wheelchair, robots in a wheelchair!" Then they all started laughing and ran back outside.

Hanna was devastated. Not that the words meant anything, because they were stupid, but they were intended to make fun of her and hurt her feelings tremendously. No one had ever made fun of her before like this and Hanna didn't know how to react. Dana took Hanna into the bathroom, where she proceeded to break down and cry. Dana hugged her and told her to ignore them, but that was easier said than done.

Amazingly, all of the teasing and hurtful things that

were said, never occurred in front of the teacher or the principal. The girls just seemed to know when they could get away with this and did the robot thing every chance they got. Interestingly, the boys never participated in the teasing, Hanna wasn't sure why. Maybe they were smarter than girls, though Hanna couldn't imagine how that could be.

A few weeks later, the Richardson family (Susie's family) took a vacation and went camping in a rented motor home. This family often babysat for Hanna, if her parents had to go away for a night or two and Jesse also babysat for their youngest child, Donna three days a week. Well unbeknownst to anyone, the camper was infested with lice. How would you even know something like that?

Jesse first noticed the problem on Donna one afternoon, while babysitting for her and when she picked up Hanna from school, she quickly checked her head. Sure enough, Hanna also had lice. Jesse had to inform the principal and keep Hanna out of school for a few days, until she could use the special medicine to wash her hair and kill the bugs. Hanna was horrified and humiliated, but even more so, when Jesse cut her hair short.

Hanna's hair hung just below her shoulders and she loved all the things Jesse could do with it; ponytails, pigtails, braids, and sometimes just hanging freely. It became so difficult for Jesse to try to comb out all of the nits (lice eggs) and decided it was easier to cut her hair short and wash all of it in a bowl of medicine. Hanna cried through the whole process. Jesse just kept assuring her that it would grow back in no time at all.

Being such a small school, of course, everyone knew and if they hadn't heard about it, Hanna's short hair was a dead giveaway. What they didn't know is that the lice came from Susie's family, not Hanna. It's just that Jesse decided to do the right thing and bring it to the attention of the school and therefore, Hanna got blamed for bringing bugs to school. It gave the kids one more thing to tease her about. It was like adding fuel to the fire.

Needless to say, her return was anything, but welcomed. The teasing got worse and most of the kids would run away from her laughing and shouting, "Cooties!" Just about everyone made fun of her for one thing or another. Almost every day, Hanna came home in tears and yet, Jesse still insisted that she figure out on her own how to make it stop. The few girls who remained friends with Hanna, didn't have a solution either.

On another occasion, Hanna had to use the restroom badly and none of the girls were willing to help her out or they weren't available. Even Dana and Vanessa were out sick, so they weren't available either. Hanna had to go so badly, that she just couldn't hold it anymore and had an accident right there in the back of the classroom. Everyone looked up at the noise and they just stared at her, as she cried her eyes out. One of the ladies from the front office took her into the bathroom and waited for Jesse to come pick her up. How would Hanna ever face her classmates again?

Jesse cleaned up the floor, while the kids were at recess and Mr. Wilson threatened them that there had better not be any teasing or anything said about this. Hanna was humiliated enough and didn't need anyone to make it worse. Of course, he wasn't aware of all the teasing that had been going on prior to this.

Somehow, Hanna managed to survive the embarrassment and just went on with school, as though nothing had happened. There was still some teasing that went on over the next couple of weeks, but Hanna decided not to be a tattletale and just tried to ignore it. Jesse still did not say a word to any of them.

Then one morning, as Jesse brought Hanna into school, Marion sat crouched in the corner by the bathroom crying because the girls were now making fun of her about something silly. Jesse got so angry and she marched into the bathroom, lined up all those little girls and gave them a talking to. She told them that if the teasing didn't stop, each of their parents would hear from her and it would not be pretty. She said they should all be ashamed of themselves. Then she stormed off and headed home.

Hanna sat there in shock! Why didn't her mom ever do that when she got teased? Hanna couldn't figure out this situation, but when she came home, she talked with her mom about it, trying to understand. Jesse explained, "You are going to have to deal with things like this your whole life and you have to be tough and know how, but the other kids don't and that's why I stepped in." Hanna still didn't quite understand this reasoning, but she trusted her mom and believed Jesse knew best.

Sometime in November, a new family moved into Fall Meadow, moving to a pig farm. There were six kids altogether and they all had their chores to do before coming to school each day. They also did not have running water, so they only bathed once a week, which meant, they smelled pretty bad. Hanna had overheard her mom talking to one of the other mothers about this family and that's how she got this information.

Margaret was one of the six children and happened to be in the sixth grade. Soon a lot of the teasing aimed at Hanna got redirected at this poor girl. Hanna knew all too well how hurtful her classmates could be and she tried to defend Margaret, but they didn't stop.

Hanna found it hard sitting close to her, because she smelled so bad, but Hanna put up with it, rather than joining the other girls and boys. Of course, that made her a target again, but at least now she wasn't alone and it was the right thing to do.

December finally arrived, as did tutoring time. Hanna actually felt relieved to have this break from going to school. She needed some time to get tough and she still had her best friends next door to visit and play with on weekends. She worried about Margaret being on her own, but figured it was like Jesse told her... Margaret had to get tough too. Meanwhile, Hanna had no plans this time, as to how to stay connected with school, but Jesse certainly did.

Just like last year, Jesse became the cheerleading mom and soon they were having practices at their house a couple times a week and going to games once a week. It surprised Kathy to learn about this, as she loved cheerleading and wanted to join the squad. Of course, Jesse would not tolerate any type of bullying or teasing between the girls and in a very short time, they were all getting along just fine, at least in terms of cheerleading...

During the cold of winter and her break from school, Hanna's parents decided to surprise her with a snowmobile ride. Mike had borrowed one from his friend at work and they thought Hanna would have a fun time. Jesse bundled her up in a snowsuit and boots, along with a ski hat, mittens and scarf. Hanna was definitely going to keep warm, though she couldn't move at all. She made quite the sight.

Mike was already on the snowmobile, straddling the back portion of the seat. Jesse carried the very padded Hanna out to the driveway, where her dad was waiting. As Jesse sat her on to the seat in front of Mike, her booted feet actually stepped down into the snow, before Jesse placed them on the sideboard. Just as Mike got ready to take off, Hanna yelled, "Wait! I want to step in the snow again!"

Somewhat puzzled, they asked her to repeat her request. They obliged and placed the bottom of her boots back down into the snow. For the first time in Hanna's life, she knew what it felt like to have the snow crunch beneath her feet. It was probably one of the most exciting things she had experienced in a very long time. Who knew?

Upon their return from the ride, Hanna requested to step in the snow one more time before going into the house. Her parents joked, "If they had known that's all it would take to get her so excited, they would not have bothered with the snowmobile, but rather they would've just brought her outside and put her feet in the snow." Sometimes, the smallest things have the greatest effect.

Hanna had a delightful Christmas, New Year's and Valentine's Day. She spent some wonderful times with her family; both sets of grandparents and her aunt. All of the good times she was having helped her forget the previous four months of her terrible experience with bullying. Her grandparents spoiled her rotten and made her feel special again. She sure did love her relatives!

With all of the cheerleading stuff going on, everything seemed to be on the mend and Hanna started looking forward to returning to school again. Jesse had always told her it takes a big person to forgive the faults of others and Hanna decided she would be a giant and forgive everyone who had been mean to her.

Hanna decided to return to school on the day before her birthday, as it was a Monday, and like last year, it worked out perfectly. There wasn't quite the celebration like before, but the following day Jesse brought a cake, which everyone shared at lunch and everyone had a nice time. Things were starting to get back to normal, though there were a few unpleasant incidents. For the most part, Hanna was okay and especially now, being 11 years old.

Just as Jesse had predicted, things did start to get better. Not all at once, but gradually the bullying finally stopped and everyone treated each other with respect, even Margaret got treated okay. Of course, the school year was almost over, but at least, every day wasn't terrible. Actually, things were getting to be like they used to be.

By the time the school year ended in May, Hanna welcomed the start of her summer. It had been a very rough year, probably the worst year of her life. She had no idea what seventh-grade would hold, but she prayed every night that it not be like this year and that she would never have another year like sixth-grade again.

Hanna did learn one very important lesson from sixth grade and it had nothing to do with her subjects… She learned that bullying is a terrible thing; it's hurtful and no one likes to be on the end of the teasing.

It's funny, because before sixth-grade, she didn't even know what being a bully meant. Hanna had started the school year with such wonderful expectations and then her bubble burst. She made a promise to herself that she would never treat anyone like that, as she knew how awful it felt. She hoped her friends had learned the same lesson.

10. Fun in the Sun

Summer was going to be different this year for Hanna, as her parents had purchased a camping trailer and they would be doing some traveling, in addition to her going to her regular summer camps. Of course, there would still be plenty of time for her and her friends to build their fort in the lilac bush, play down by the treehouse, go to the lake, do some fishing under the bridge and hang out in town by the little store.

Things were changing though and Hanna wasn't quite sure why. Some of her friends were busy with family time, going on their own vacations, while others made new friends with whom they hung out and it seemed as though their interests were different than before. Hanna figured it probably had to do with everyone growing up and it was common for these things to happen. She was absolutely right.

Hanna being only 11 years old, wasn't all that grown up or anything, but the last school year made her realize not everything in the world is always good. That particular lesson made her grow up a little bit more than she probably would have, if nothing like that ever happened to her. Hanna hoped any future lessons would not be so difficult, as she didn't like this one at all, but she knew growing up wasn't going to be easy.

Hanna decided that she would always do her best to treat everyone kindly, be honest and do her best to understand why people did the things they did. Maybe she would grow up to be a psychiatrist (a special doctor for problems with the mind) and work on figuring out people's behaviors. Debbie's mother was a psychiatrist and made lots of money. Then again, she wanted to be an animal doctor- a veterinarian, because she loved animals and they made lots of money too. Then again, she might just decide to become a teacher.

Of course, money was not the most important thing, but in Hanna's case, she would always need someone to take care of her and that would cost lots of money. So she wanted a job she liked and made a lot of money, but she guessed most people had that same wish. Nobody wanted to work a job they didn't like and she was pretty sure they didn't want to do it for free, so she would have to do well in school to get the job she wanted.

She had been trying to talk her parents into getting a dog for years, but they always said no. They would tell her they were too busy to care for the dog and since Hanna couldn't do the care, it just wasn't an option. That made her sad, but she understood how hard her parents worked and didn't want to give them any extra jobs.

However, all of Hanna's friends had a pet; many of them had a dog, some had kitties, one of them had a rabbit, another a bird and Marge had a horse. Of course, she lived on a farm, but still, Hanna wanted a dog. She was very jealous of her friends in regard to pets. It's funny, she wasn't jealous about everyone else being able to walk. Hanna thought to herself, "Maybe someday…"

The first few weeks of summer went by so quickly. Hanna couldn't believe it when she looked at the calendar and saw today's date of June 23. Another week and she would be traveling. Hanna and all of her friends had been having a grand old time so far. She even had fun helping Dana pull weeds in the garden, which was one of Dana's weekly chores. Hanna loved helping her friends whenever she could, because they were always helping her.

Now pulling weeds proved to be no easy task for Hanna. Dana would take her out of her chair (her stroller) and sit her on the ground right in front of her. Hanna would grab a weed, hold onto it tightly and throw her body back into Dana's lap, landing with a thud and weed in hand. Using her body weight was the only thing making her strong enough to do this. Dana would then push her back up to restart the process, all the while pulling her own weeds around her. They were quite the team.

A week later, Hanna was getting packed and going on vacation to South Dakota. She decided to take her friend Marion along, instead of Dana or Vanessa, because they had been getting to be good friends and her neighborhood pals were going somewhere with their own family.

Marion couldn't be more thrilled that Hanna had invited her and continuously apologized for her actions during the last school year. Hanna completely forgave her. She put that behind her and they were going to have fun.

Hanna was excited about this particular vacation. She and her family had camped before, but this time they had a new travel trailer with a built in kitchen, a dinette and a bathroom. She felt happiest about the bathroom because Hanna hated using the outhouse. They always smelled so bad and there were too many bugs. Hanna feared that one of them would bite her on her butt!

The drive to South Dakota took a long time with hot temperatures, but they eventually came to some pretty cool areas. They visited a place called "Wall Drug," a giant drugstore with all kinds of mechanical dolls and statues and they had fun. The best part for her was the root beer floats they drank to cool off.

Marion taught Hanna some new road games to play; tracking how many license plates they could spot, doing an alphabet game using road signs and a couple of memory games. Hanna taught Marion a bunch of new card games, and they were always in some type of competition. Not a mean kind, just a good friendly kind.

Marion and Hanna enjoyed many of the same things, which made it especially nice having her along on this trip. They traded clothes, as they were the same size, they fixed each other's hair, they liked the same kind of music, often singing along to the radio and they loved teasing Hanna's dad. Of course, he enjoyed teasing them right back, especially when it came to their singing.

Marion and Hanna also enjoyed talking in a southern accent and acting out skits. They would make up stories and then record themselves on Hanna's tape recorder. They could do this for hours and then they would listen to themselves and crack-up laughing at how silly they sounded. Needless to say, they were never bored.

They traveled through the "Badlands," visited "Mount Rushmore" and camped near Deadwood City, which was an old western town. Counting the days of driving, they were gone for about a week, visiting different sites each day and sitting around the campfire at night. Hanna had a wonderful time with Marion.

The Badlands were some weird looking mountains

with barren land all around. You wouldn't want to get stuck out there, that's for sure. Mount Rushmore was the famous president's heads carved into the mountain and they were amazing. Hanna could not figure out how anyone could have done that work. Deadwood City was known as the place where Wild Bill Hickok died in a poker game. Can you imagine getting killed over a card game? The whole trip turned into a fun history lesson. Too bad all history lessons couldn't be this fun!

They also celebrated the Fourth of July, while on vacation, which included a big fireworks show at the lake near the campground they were staying in. Hanna loved fireworks, especially the ones that came down like Weeping Willow trees. Jesse had packed hot chocolate and all kinds of snacks to munch on, as they watched the beautiful colors and helped America celebrate her birthday. Hanna thought it might be fun to have fireworks to celebrate her birthday!

When they weren't exploring new places, they would spend time at the lake swimming, picnicking and relaxing. Hanna's parents were never too far away, but yet, they let Hanna and Marion have their private time. Usually while the girls were sunbathing, Mike spent some time fishing and Jesse enjoyed reading. Everyone was having a good time.

One of the last excursions they took landed them in a place called "Flintstone City" and it looked just like the cartoon on TV. The buildings seemed like they were made out of rock and there were two cars with no outer bodies, just the frame, axle and big tires. One looked like Fred's car and the other just like Barney's. It was a cool place, kind of like being on TV.

Hanna felt sad when their vacation ended, but she couldn't help but be excited too, because she would be going to her other camps soon. Of course, she still had three weeks before then and she was going to make the best of it.

She spent the rest of July with friends, doing all the things they liked doing over the summer. They say, "Time Flies When You're Having Fun" and it certainly did. She couldn't believe August was just a few days away.

Hanna spent the whole month of August at summer camp. She had one week at the MDA camp, located in Michigan, a good couple hour drive from her hometown and then three weeks at Peacock camp, just a short distance away from her actual house. As with previous years, Hanna had an incredible time at both places.

Nancy made it back for another year as Hanna's counselor and Hanna was thrilled, though she knew too well this would probably be their last year together. Even though they only saw one another for one week each year, they were surprisingly good friends. Matter of fact, Nancy invited Hanna to come to her house and stay for a week around Halloween and Hanna didn't hesitate to accept!

Most of her friends from Peacock camp were there again and she learned some actual sign language this time around. Not just the regular alphabet, but real words. She again, won the floating contest and her dorm room won for the best skit. All in all, it was a very good year for going to camp.

She loved the time away from home, the independence, all of the cool activities, seeing old friends and making new ones and like years gone by, Hanna still felt heartbroken when the time came to say goodbye. Of course, she was comforted by knowing she would be back next summer and seventh grade would begin in only a few days.

Hanna's emotions were like riding a roller coaster, excited one minute to be going somewhere new or doing something special and then having it come to an end or having to say goodbye to someone close, making her sad.

Her whole summer had been like that; happy when school ended, but sad to say goodbye to some of her friends, happy to spend a few weeks with her neighborhood friends, but sad to leave them behind to go on vacation, happy to go on vacation, but sad when it ended, happy to go to summer camp, but sad when each of them came to a close. Thank goodness her summer was almost over. All these up-and-down feelings made her tired.

Hanna's summer ended with some school shopping for clothes and school supplies. This time, she just went with Jesse and no friends. She bought several new outfits, new shoes and most exciting, a new bra. Jesse insisted she didn't need one, but all of Hanna's friends were wearing them now and she wanted one too.

Jesse figured she would only be in a training bra, but was surprised when Hanna's size turned out to be a 30 AA. She couldn't deny that Hanna was starting to develop into a young woman. It made Jesse feel old… Her baby was growing up.

Then they attended the annual Fall Meadow Labor Day picnic/BBQ and had a good time. Everyone got together bringing something to the party and it turned out to be a wonderful end of summer celebration. All of her friends sat around talking about the beginning of school with no mention of the horrors of sixth grade. Hanna had high hopes for the upcoming year.

The following day was the day before school, which meant Hanna had to decide what to wear and how she would wear her hair, along with what special lunch she would bring. She spent most of her day in preparation for the following morning, including putting her backpack together and talking on the phone to several of her friends.

Hanna went to bed early to get a good night's sleep, as she wanted to be bright eyed and bushy tailed for her big day. She was excited and had a good feeling about this upcoming school year. It would be the best year ever, she was absolutely sure of it!

11. Maturity Begins to Set in

Hanna opened her eyes and just like last year, she tried to pretend she didn't feel nervous or excited about this first day of school. She had decided to have Jesse set her alarm clock because that's what her friends did to make sure they were up on time. Of course, Hanna woke up a good 15 minutes early and her mom showed up before the alarm started ringing, but it was the principle of the thing.

Hanna wasn't quite so talkative this morning, as she had been the previous two years. Of course, back then she anticipated some wonderful times and could hardly contain her feelings. Whereas, today was somewhat different because Hanna didn't quite know what to expect.

She wondered if the bullying was completely over; would everyone get along and treat each other nicely without teasing? Hanna pushed those thoughts out of her head for the moment and told Jesse what outfit she wanted to wear. They had already gone through the bathroom, corset and underwear routine without much conversation.

Hanna chose a summery, sleeveless, flowery print

dress, with an A-line style about an inch above her knee in length. She wore her white patent leather flats with no socks and felt very grown-up with this choice. She let her hair hang long, which hung just above her shoulders, since her hair cut last year with her bangs being the perfect length.

Once Hanna finished getting up and dressed, she used her wheelchair this particular morning for breakfast and brushing her teeth in the bathroom, before it got relocated back to the teacher's lounge for the week. She didn't have much of an appetite this morning, but forced herself to eat a piece of toast with peanut butter and a banana. The last thing she needed was to feel weak her first day back to school.

The rest of the routine happened as it had for the previous two grades; Jesse carried Hanna out to the car, put on her seat belt, as Dana and Vanessa came running across the front yard from their house. They hopped in, while Jesse loaded the wheelchair into the trunk.

They were also quiet and Jesse knew they all had concerns about how the day would go. She was quite touched by how much these girls cared about her daughter and did their best to protect her. She had some precious cargo in this vehicle.

Upon their arrival at school, Jesse took Hanna's wheelchair to the top of the stairs, then carried Hanna to her throne and kissed her goodbye, wishing her a good day. The three girls walked to their classroom, as this year they would all be together; Vanessa in sixth grade, Hanna in seventh grade and Dana in eighth grade. They were once again, "The Three Musketeers," as Hanna's dad often, affectionately called them.

As they proceeded down the hall, they were greeted by several of the other girls, including Kathy and

Margaret. Everyone chattered and giggled happily, as they strolled the rest of the way to their classroom. Things were looking good. They entered the room and were welcomed by Mr. Wilson again. He remained as the upperclassman teacher, which made Hanna happy because he was very nice.

Vanessa had been pushing Hanna this time and parked her at her desk, which had been set up by her dad before the holiday weekend. Rather than being off to one side of the classroom, Hanna now sat directly behind the two middle rows; the seventh grade rows. She liked having the sixth graders on her right and the eighth-graders on the left near the windows. They got to sit by the windows because they had priority. Next year, Hanna would have that privilege.

Hanna removed her new school supplies from her backpack and organized them "just so," making her desk comfortable and feeling like home. She was ready to begin the new school year. Everyone else clambered for what they considered to be the best seat and everyone found their place when the bell rang.

Mr. Wilson must've been in a good mood because he let everyone sit in the desk they had selected. That started the day out well for everyone. He first did his usual introduction and then went on and passed out their books. Each of the subjects were exactly the same as last year, except that they were in a different order and of course, a level higher, making them a little more difficult.

All of the hard subjects were still before lunch and they occurred this way to prevent them from happening along with the other two grades. So her day started with penmanship, which gave her brain time to wake up and be ready to learn. She had been doing cursive for enough years that it became just a habit now.

Her next subject was math, followed by science and then recess. Hanna decided to be very brave and asked Kathy if she wanted to stay in with her. To her pleasant surprise, Kathy agreed. They spent the 15 minutes talking about their summer vacation and you would've never known that there had been any bullying or teasing. Hanna felt elated!

Once the bell rang and everyone back in their seats, they moved on to social studies, Hanna's least favorite subject. This year they were going to be learning about other countries and that would probably be more interesting, she thought. Spelling and vocabulary were next, the easiest subject for Hanna… She was a natural at spelling.

The last subject before lunch was English and of course, Mr. Wilson had them write an essay about what they did over summer vacation. Writing the paper was easy and the hard part was figuring out what part of the summer she wanted to share. She finally made up her mind and decided on her vacation to South Dakota.

Soon they were all at lunch, sitting at the same table, trading with one another and having a good time. Hanna was happy to be back at school and even happier to have everything back to what it used to be. She figured it must be because they were all growing up and maturing a little bit.

After lunch, her subjects were exactly the same as last year and in the same order, as music/art and PE were taught the same to all three grades by the same teachers. Hanna loved this set up because she, Dana and Vanessa could work together on the same art project. During PE, Hanna cheered her classmates on, as the girls played a friendly game of basketball.

When Jesse picked the girls up from school, she

knew immediately that things had gone well. Hanna had a grin from ear to ear and they were each talking a mile a minute, trying to share their day, all at the same time. Dana returned Hanna's wheelchair to the teacher's lounge and hurried back to the car.

Hanna talked a lot through dinner, telling her dad all about her day and Jesse smiled, knowing that Hanna had overcome one of her first big hurdles in her young life and she had done it with grace and charm. Jesse couldn't be prouder... She knew her daughter had a wonderful future ahead of her.

Hanna did her homework quickly because there wasn't much to do. Mr. Wilson must've stayed in his good mood because he didn't assign much at all. Hanna went to bed early; not only because she felt tired, but because she wanted tomorrow to get here quickly. She was back to looking forward to going to school.

The first month of school just flew by and pretty soon they were into October. Autumn had definitely arrived with all of the changing colors and cooler temperatures. The first dance of the year was coming up and for the first time, Hanna decided to attend. She considered herself too young last year and had no interest in dancing, but now, she was beginning to notice the boys in her class and enjoyed the thought of having a boyfriend someday.

So the big weekend finally arrived and Hanna attended the dance with several of her girlfriends, including Debbie, Susie, Dana and Kathy. Vanessa declined to participate, as she wasn't into boys or dancing yet. Jesse allowed Hanna to wear a little bit of lipstick and some perfume to accent her outfit. She wore a short plaid skirt, a striped blouse and knee-high boots. She was quite fashionable, even if she did say so herself.

The band happened to be a local group with four guys from the high school. The lights were low and chairs were set up around the perimeter of the gym, which is where the dance was held, of course. Slowly but surely, the boys moseyed over to where the girls were hanging out and one by one, they were asked to dance. When they weren't asked by one of the boys, the girls would usually dance with each other. It seemed funny to Hanna that it was okay for the girls to dance together, but not the boys. How sad for them.

As the evening drew to an end, Hanna was losing all hope that any of her male classmates would ask her to dance. As the band played their closing number, Hanna knew her inklings were right. She had Dana push her to the girls' bathroom and she just started crying. Her heart was breaking and for the first time in a long time, Hanna felt she wasn't like everyone else. Within a few minutes, Jesse found her daughter and tried to console her.

She got Hanna and Dana into the car and on the way home, she explained, "At this age, boys have difficulty asking any girl to dance, let alone someone in a wheelchair. It takes a lot of courage for these boys because they're afraid of being rejected, just like you're afraid of no one asking you to dance. It's only going to take one boy to break the ice and the others will follow. I promise you, things will get better!"

The next few weeks passed by and soon it was Halloween. Hanna went to the city to stay with her friend/counselor, Nancy from MDA camp, for the Halloween weekend and she had a delightful time. Jesse dropped her off Saturday morning and would pick her up Sunday evening. Later that morning, Nancy took her to get a manicure, the first one she'd ever had and she felt so grown up.

They went to a costume party put on by the MDA organization on Saturday afternoon and Hanna dressed as a hippy. Her costume included flowered bellbottoms with a polka dot shirt in bright orange and yellow colors. She had flowers painted on her face and wore big hot pink sunglasses. They had lots of goodies, played games and had a lot of fun.

This was the first time Hanna had ever been out on Halloween. Usually, Dana, Vanessa and Paul would come to her house to get dressed up and then they would go out trick-or-treating, including a bag for Hanna. She would get dressed up too, but it was always too cold after dark for her to go outside, so she would stay back and answer the door for the other trick-or-treaters. She very much enjoyed getting to go to the party. She knew her neighbors had a good time too.

Nancy and Hanna stayed up late Saturday night, answering the door for the trick-or-treaters and then watched scary movies, ate popcorn and had a good old time. Sunday morning they slept in, had breakfast at lunch time and all too soon, Jesse arrived to take Hanna home. She and Nancy agreed to do this again sometime soon before summer camp.

During the month of November, another dance occurred down the street from MEADOWGREEN Elementary at St. Mary's Catholic school. They didn't have a gymnasium, but they did have a basement and that's where they held their dance. Same band as the last dance and pretty much the same kids. Hanna was not expecting to dance, setting her expectations lower, so as not to be disappointed.

To Hanna's utter amazement, she did get asked to dance. Susie's older brother, Joey, came right up and asked her first thing. She couldn't believe it, but she could say yes. She rolled herself out onto the dance floor and moving her body from the waist up, jerking her arms and such, Hanna danced her first dance with a boy. She just wanted to scream with excitement!

Now Hanna thought to herself, "Did Susie pay him or bribe him in some other way?" Then she decided, it didn't matter because soon the other boys in her class were also asking her to dance. So whatever the reason, Jesse turned out to be absolutely right. It only took one boy to break the ice and now, Hanna was being asked to dance just like all the other girls. It was turning out to be a very good year.

The school year continued on and surprisingly, they had a very mild winter. So Hanna had her regular Christmas break like everyone else, but the powers that be decided if the weather continued to be this mild, Hanna could stay in school and not have to have winter tutoring. She excitedly welcomed the notion of skipping tutoring!

As if things could get any better, Hanna got the surprise of a lifetime. When she woke up Christmas morning, Mike carried her out to the couch and a box under the tree started to move on its own with a whining noise coming from inside. Mike picked up the box, took off the lid and there staring up at her was the cutest little black puppy she had ever seen. Mike quickly lifted the little guy from the box and placed him in Hanna's lap.

Hanna started to cry, not because she felt sad, but because this is how she showed her happiness and the puppy did his best to lick her tears away. Mike and Jesse stood by and said, "Merry Christmas Hanna!" Her tears quickly turned to laughter and she kept saying, "Thank You, Thank You, Thank You!" Jessie asked her what she would name him and Hanna quickly replied, "Baby, because he's my baby."

It took a few weeks, but eventually Mike had Baby house broken and he already knew commands like sit, stay and lay down, as well as the word "No." Hanna loved her dog and Baby appeared to love her back. In no time at all, they were inseparable, except of course, when Hanna attended school or somewhere else where dogs weren't allowed.

Hanna didn't think life could get any better... Not a bad place to be for an 11, soon to be 12-year-old. Before long, the weather started to warm up and just like last year, Jesse volunteered to be the team mom for the cheerleaders for basketball and baseball. She declined the job during football season, but Debbie's mom stepped in for that one and Hanna still got to be part of the gang.

Baby attended most of the games with Hanna and had begun to grow quite large. He grew to be a beautiful solid black Labrador retriever and extremely smart. Not only was he intelligent, but also well behaved and loving.

Hanna's birthday fell on Thursday this year, so Hanna held her first slumber party on the day after. Jesse and Mike went out for the evening, leaving the eight young ladies on their own for about two hours protected by Baby. He was a great watchdog, though there wasn't much to guard in Fall Meadow.

Dana, Vanessa, Susie, Marion, Debbie, Kathy, Marge and Hanna had a ball. They played games, listened to music, put on makeup, ate way too many snacks and by the time Hanna's parents got home, the girls were all fired up. It was going to be a long night for Jesse and Mike and they were thankful this only happened once a year.

Sometime in April, a couple of the girls were hanging out in the girl's bathroom during recess, something they should not have been doing, but we all do things we shouldn't. They were all getting along quite well now and generally stayed together, so this was not an uncommon occurrence.

Hanna was leaning forward in her chair, while Marge stood on the little bars in the back, which usually aid in tipping the wheelchair back. Neither of the girls were thinking about the consequence of the situation and as Marge stood on them with all of her weight, the chair tipped back, causing Hanna's body to fall back with her weight knocking the chair right out of Marge's hands. This resulted in Hanna's head hitting the marble floor. Marge, one of the most sweet and mild-mannered of them all was devastated at hurting her friend.

Hanna was immediately knocked unconscious and when the girls sat her chair back up, Dana instinctively started to gently slap her face and call her name. Within a few seconds, Hanna opened her eyes with her head throbbing terribly. Marge had run to the office to call Jesse immediately.

The only thing Hanna remembered was her whole body went numb, feeling all tingly everywhere and then the next thing she knew Dana was slapping her and calling her name. She had a huge bump on the back of her head and Jesse in somewhat of a state of panic, snatched Hanna from her wheelchair and headed for the emergency room in the nearby town of McHenry. Poor Jesse had to drive using one hand because she had to balance Hanna's head with the other to keep it from touching the seat.

Once at the hospital, Hanna was examined for a concussion, but they were pretty sure she wouldn't have one because of the lump on her head. They explained that usually a concussion results with a dent in the skull, rather than a big goose egg. They did however, stress to

Jesse to watch Hanna over the next eight hours and make sure that her eyes didn't dilate. They suggested she not go to sleep for the same amount of time. Hanna had a major headache, but nothing else.

Hanna had survived quite a few injuries throughout her young life. One time, while Jesse carried her out of Mary Ellen's house, she slipped on a throw rug above the basement stairs and they rode down together like a surfboard with Jesse losing Hanna from her arms at the end. Hanna landed on her arm, causing a fracture and had her lower tooth puncture her upper lip, requiring several stitches. Thankfully, her head landed on a pile of newspapers, instead of the concrete floor.

There were numerous occasions when Jesse would carry Hanna in the wintertime, walking on ice, slipping and landing on one of Hanna's ankles, resulting in a fairly severe sprain. One time Dana tried to sit her up on the bed and twisted her ankle causing another pretty bad sprain. There were countless times Hanna got her head bumped on a doorway when she was carried from one room to another. Jesse just couldn't get used to her length as she began to grow. Luckily, none of the injuries proved to be too serious... Hanna was a pretty tough cookie!

All of the sudden, May showed up on the calendar and there were only a couple of weeks left to the school year. One morning, Hanna woke up and didn't feel very good, so Jesse let her stay home from school, as Hanna had never faked illness before. She spent most of her day watching TV, as she especially liked the game shows.

While lying in bed that afternoon, watching the Newlywed game, suffering mostly from a headache and stomach cramps, Jesse and Hanna discovered why she wasn't feeling very well. Hanna's body, just like the girls attitudes was maturing and she was entering puberty.

This is a time when all young people begin their journey into adulthood. Jesse's little girl was growing into a young lady and she couldn't be more proud, but she felt sad too, as she was losing her little girl.

Seventh grade came to an end and it had been quite the eventful year for Hanna. She danced with a boy for the first time, went to her first Halloween party, stayed in school all year without any tutoring, got a puppy, turned 12 years old and started developing into a young woman.

Hanna continued to grow and learn about herself, as well as others and continued to do quite well at navigating the world around her from MEADOWGREEN Elementary School to the town of Fall Meadow and beyond… Hanna's world was expanding, as was her understanding of life.

12. Sitting on Top of the World

The summer between seventh and eighth grade progressed pretty similarly to the past couple of summer breaks. Hanna spent time with her neighborhood friends, though now, some of her other school friends were coming over and hanging out a good part of the time. They all continued to play down by the treehouse, fish under the bridge and spend time in town, meeting up with others, while coming up with different things to do.

The Catholic school closed at the end of seventh grade, so some of the kids would be attending MEADOWGREEN, while others would go to schools closer to their homes. Carol was one of the new girls and Hanna liked her a lot. They met at her friend Debbie's, as they were neighbors and Hanna looked forward to Carol being a classmate.

Baby had grown now to full size and reminded her of a big teddy bear. He was extremely lovable and very gentle around Hanna, as if he knew something was different about her. He never stepped on her or put his full weight on her in any way. He listened to her every command, always making sure to be in earshot of her call.

He also kept himself close to her so she could pet him. He was an amazing dog and Hanna couldn't imagine her life without him.

Hanna's family went on another vacation with their camper and this time, they went to Virginia to visit her dad's cousins. Vanessa came along as Hanna's companion and they had a wonderful time. They camped along the way and finally reached their destination after several days. They saw all kinds of neat things during their journey and Baby proved to be a very good traveler, as well. Hanna always felt safe with her protector nearby.

Several of Hanna's cousins were very good-looking and Vanessa developed a crush almost as soon as they got there. It was a short-lived romance, as they were only there for a week, but Jimmy seemed to like her back and they agreed to keep in touch. Hanna knew that it would never work because she would hardly ever write or call her friends from camp and she liked them a lot too.

The week passed by quickly and soon they were on their drive home. They didn't make as many stops and managed to get home after just two days. Of course, Mike drove very long days and the girls slept through a big part of it. Hanna had to admit, she was glad to be home.

Once they were home, Hanna went to her traditional month of summer camp; one week at the MDA camp and three weeks at Peacock camp. Of course, Hanna like always, felt very excited to be going, but sadly, she had to leave Baby behind and that created a new unpleasant part about going to camp, not just leaving her neighborhood friends.

Well, there was one other new thing; though completely expected, Nancy could not there as Hanna's counselor and that made Hanna very sad. Nancy had been working a regular job since the end of last summer, saving her money and getting ready to start college. Hanna would miss her a lot, though she understood completely! Everyone grows up and has to do what's right for their life.

Hanna's new counselor, Tina was only 15 years old, three years older than Hanna. Hanna liked having her so close in age, as it made it easy to become very good friends. She was very nice and more like a sister than a babysitter or mother figure. Not that Nancy ever acted like that, but the seven years difference definitely made her the boss.

Camp turned out to be as wonderful as it always did, but as usual, it was difficult to say goodbye at the end. Tina and Hanna promised to keep in touch and request one another for the following year. They cried almost the whole bus ride home, but Hanna knew she would be off to Peacock camp in another day or so and all of this sadness would be behind her. Hanna enjoyed having a full summer.

After spending a delightful three weeks with old friends and new ones at camp Peacock, she and her family spent Labor Day weekend shopping for school and then celebrating the end of the summer at the annual Fall Meadow picnic. Hanna couldn't believe she was about to begin eighth-grade. Just four years ago, Hanna had never gone to school, let alone being one of the top dogs, and she never imagined how cool it could be.

The first day of school started like every other one… Hanna woke up long before her alarm clock went off and Jesse came through her door. Hanna was feeling on top of the world this particular morning. The bullying had become a faded memory, she had many friends, she no longer had winter tutoring, she had a wonderful pet and most importantly, she was an eighth grader!

Today, Hanna didn't dress like a little girl… Instead, she wore a flowered print miniskirt, a short sleeved white blouse and a lightweight vest of the same print as her skirt. She wore pantyhose, even though it was kind of hot outside with a pair of white pumps, which had a very low heel. Baby stayed back out of the way, but watched the whole process of getting Hanna up and dressed.

Without much discussion, other than all the things Hanna planned for the day, Jesse had her in her brace, used the restroom, panties, nylons, skirt and shoes on and then in her chair ready for the top half. In just a few more minutes, Hanna had her bra, shirt and vest situated, ready for the next step of her morning routine.

Her hair had grown quite long now, down past her shoulders and she just let it hang freely, parted down the middle. Her bangs had grown out considerably too, long enough to pull behind her ears and that's how she liked it. In another 20 minutes, she had eaten, brushed her teeth, packed her backpack and headed out the door.

Baby trotted out alongside them and waited his turn to jump into the back seat. He had gotten quite used to the routine of travel and was very excited about going for a ride, though he would not be very happy when he didn't get to stay with Hanna at school. Hanna envied students who were blind and could keep their guide dogs always at their side. Not that Hanna wanted to be blind, she just wanted Baby always at her side.

Vanessa came running across her yard to hitch a ride, but it would only be her this year because Dana graduated last year and went on to high school. The high school was five miles away, so Dana had to ride the bus like most of the kids in town. Next year, they could drive together once again, but for now, Hanna was content to have Vanessa as a travel buddy. They jabbered nonstop, all the while Jesse loaded the wheelchair and until they arrived at school.

Once inside, everybody visited with everybody, as they made their way to their classroom. Hanna was excited because her eighth-grade class would be next to the windows this year and she liked being able to look outside when she wasn't doing something else. It proved to be a very nice privilege for the eighth-graders.

Now that the Catholic school had closed and quite a few kids transferred over, the classroom was quite crowded. Rumor had it that there would be a new addition to the school and each class would have their own room. That would be very cool.

The school year progressed quickly and without much drama. Each day, Hanna would have a different friend assist her during lunch and recess and there were a number of girls who could help her use the restroom. She no longer had any problems with any of her classmates and school dances were always fun, never leaving her without someone to dance with.

As an eighth grader, Hanna's class were given priority for most things and Hanna liked her new position. She certainly felt as though she was on top of the world! Her classes were not difficult, she had a straight "A" report card and she couldn't imagine things getting any better. Other than having to leave Baby every day, life was more than perfect.

By Christmas time, Hanna was doing well and the mild winter allowed her to skip winter tutoring once again. Staying in school, on the same schedule as everyone else made her very happy. Once again, her mother became involved with the cheerleaders for basketball and baseball season, allowing her to be in the thick of things. It's funny how initially, this was her scheme to stay involved with everyone and now, it had become just another routine. Hanna loved her routines.

Each day after school, Vanessa would push Hanna to the front door and Jesse would be waiting in the car right up front. As soon as Hanna saw the car, she broke into a great big smile because there sat Baby in the backseat, anxiously waiting for her. As soon as Jesse put Hanna in the front seat, Baby would lean over and give her lots of kisses, while Jesse buckled her in.

Then it was Vanessa's turn for kisses... As she crawled into the backseat, after getting Hanna's chair to the office, Baby gave her a fair share of affection. Hanna felt sure that Baby considered Vanessa as one of the family and Vanessa thought of him just like her own pet. They all loved each other very much.

Hanna didn't go to Nancy's this year for Halloween because she was away at college, which is not one of the holidays they got off. Hanna felt sad about not seeing Nancy, especially after missing her this past summer at camp, but it was all part of growing up and moving on. Hanna wasn't sure she liked that part of growing up.

This year, they had a Halloween dance at school and Hanna dressed up as a devil. Everyone thought it to be kind of a funny choice because Hanna was pretty much an angel most of the time. Everyone wore a costume and had a lot of fun. After the dance, her friends still went trick-or-treating and brought her a big bag of goodies, while she answered the door, passing out candy to the other trick-or-treaters.

It was sometime in November when they learned for sure about the new addition to their school. They were so excited. There would be two stories at the end of their building; the lower level would house the new cafeteria, the library, a Media Center and the kindergarten, whereas the upper level would have four classrooms for the fifth through eighth grades.

First through fourth grades would remain on the main level in the original classrooms. The plan was to have it completed before everyone returned from Christmas break. Hanna couldn't wait!

The holiday came and went. As usual, Hanna got together with her whole family and had a wonderful time. Of course, this year she didn't get a puppy, so it wasn't quite as exciting as last year, but she still got some pretty cool gifts. Mostly clothes, music and a cassette tape recorder. She didn't get any toys this year, as she was starting to outgrow playing with Barbie and there wasn't much else she actually played with.

Baby had been with Hanna for a year now and had grown to be quite the beautiful Labrador and so very well behaved. He had celebrated his first birthday two weeks before Thanksgiving, but Christmas marked their anniversary, so Hanna bought him a new play toy and some yummy dog treats. Hanna could not remember a time when she was without Baby at her side.

One other exciting thing happened over Christmas break; Hanna got fitted for a new motorized wheelchair. They took all of her measurements, which included the height from her knees to her feet in order to place the foot pedals correctly. The armrests were measured, the control box and her headrest all had to be perfectly placed. They were expecting she would have it sometime early May and Hanna hoped to have it before graduation.

Luckily, the winter wasn't too bad and the snow didn't keep Hanna home bound for the entire two weeks of her Christmas break. She actually got to go to the movies a couple of times with her friends and also did some shopping. In no time at all, her Christmas break ended and it was time to return to school. The kids had heard that the construction was complete other than a few minor details. Hanna couldn't wait to see her new classroom.

Their first day back happened just like any other day… Jesse drove, Hanna sat next to her in the front seat and Vanessa, along with Baby, sat in the back. They arrived with time to spare, but when they arrived, things weren't as Hanna expected. After Jesse took in her chair and then Hanna, they were met by Mr. Risner, which worried Hanna considerably.

Mr. Risner had them come into his office together, and gently broke the news… In all of the planning, no one had thought about Hanna and her wheelchair in regards to the new classroom upstairs. The school now three levels, had no elevator. Not only wouldn't she be able to get to her new classroom, but the cafeteria, as well as the new library, were out of her reach. Hanna felt as though she'd just been kicked in the gut.

Mr. Risner went on to explain that the classroom wouldn't be a problem because they would just keep the eighth-graders on the main level, but lunchtime and library time would prove to be a bit more difficult.

For Hanna, there would be no opportunity to try out any of the new equipment downstairs and instead of watching movies on the new screen, they were going to have to resort to using the gym for such things. Hanna was not happy about any of this and she knew her classmates were going to be just as sad.

As for lunch, one of Hanna's friends would have to go down to the cafeteria and get their hot lunch or buy items from the vending machines and then they would have to eat in the classroom by themselves. Hanna would no longer have the opportunity of trading lunch and spending time with all of her friends together, which had always been one of her favorite things to do. Hanna wanted to cry, but thought to herself, "I'm too old to cry!"

There was a great deal of confusion when the bell rang because the fifth through eighth graders went running up the stairs, only to find that the fourth through seventh graders were located up there. The eighth-graders quickly learned that they were still on the main floor, in the same old classroom, surrounded by the baby grades. They were anything, but happy and of course, it seemed to be all Hanna's fault. She knew they were a lot more than sad... They were mad and upset!

Mr. Wilson had made the decision to teach eighth-grade, so two other teachers were hired for the sixth and seventh grades. For that matter, five new teachers were hired to cover the separation of all of the grades. MEADOWGREEN Elementary was growing in leaps and bounds.

Once they were inside their old classroom, the same one as they had been prior to Christmas vacation, everyone found their seat. Though they enjoyed all the extra space around them, they were still mad. None of them were happy with the old, tattered room, knowing that everything upstairs was brand new and shiny. Everyone felt down in the dumps and didn't even smile at Hanna. All she could think about; "Here we go again!" Of course, this time, it included both the boys and girls.

Just like everything else, they eventually, got over it. Matter of fact, having all the little kids on the same floor made them feel older and more in charge. All those lower grades looked up to them and they were in awe of the eighth-graders. The eighth-graders ate it up.

Everyone came to realize it was just one of those things and it wasn't Hanna's fault. She didn't do it intentionally and like anything new, little problems kept popping up in the upstairs classrooms; the speakers didn't always work, sometimes the lights would flicker and on rare occasion the heater wouldn't keep the rooms warm, which only goes to prove sometimes, things happen for the best.

By early February, everyone had settled in to their new location and the addition seemed like it had always been there. The excitement wore off, while the new routines became commonplace and school became just school. Everyone turned their attention to springtime, when the weather warmed up and playing outdoors was an option.

Soon March arrived and Hanna turned 13 years old making her a teenager now. She certainly enjoyed the whole concept. Her aunt gave her a bottle of Chanel #5 cologne because she said every young woman should have a special perfume. Hanna knew how expensive that perfume was and decided to only wear it on very special occasions. She was growing up.

This year, her birthday happened to fall on a Friday and she had a slumber party to celebrate. Jesse had agreed to 10 guests this time and like last year, her and Mike disappeared for most of the evening. Hanna couldn't blame them; who would want to hang out with a bunch of young teenage girls if they weren't one themselves... Well maybe teenage boys? Baby loved all of the attention from the girls!

The rest of the year seemed to fly by and soon there was only a couple weeks of school left with graduation being held on May 16. The last week of school proved to be very exciting! Her class didn't do any more schoolwork, as they had completed their textbooks, took their final tests and spent the rest of the time rehearsing for her graduation ceremony. During the same time, Hanna's motorized wheelchair arrived.

The first couple times she tried to drive it was anything, but pretty. Hanna had a hard time getting it to go in a straight line and wound up in the flower bed a couple of times, but after a few days, she was a pro! Her dad used their truck to bring the chair to the school on Wednesday, May 14, so she could have some time to practice for the ceremony.

Hanna had discovered a whole new freedom... She experienced a thrill like never before with her new independence and loved being able to go where she wanted to go, when she wanted to, without having to ask someone to take her there. Hanna was in heaven!

In addition to rehearsal and wheelchair practice, Hanna also went shopping for her graduation dress. Her mom found a beautiful silver sparkly dress, which was actually designed as a wraparound, fastening in the front with a low, plunging neckline. Jesse, a very good seamstress, altered the dress to fit Hanna perfectly. She turned it around backwards, making it Empire style with the v-neckline on her back. It turned out quite lovely. She chose a pair of white patent leather pumps for her shoes, which complemented her dress nicely.

The morning of graduation day, the eighth-graders didn't have to come in, so they could do the necessary preparations for the evening festivities. Hanna went to their family friend who was also a hairdresser. Jimmy always did Hanna's haircuts and stuff, but this time he was actually doing a fancy hairstyle.

Hanna didn't sleep well the night before and was exhausted before the day even started. She fell asleep while Jimmy washed her hair and set it. After an hour under the dryer, Jimmy took out the rollers and her hair hung perfectly straight. Hanna was devastated… Why did that happen and now what was she going to do?

Jimmy explained that her hair was too long and heavy and that's why it wouldn't hold the curl. He told her not to worry and within a couple of minutes, he placed a "fall" on her head. A fall is like a partial wig; rather than covering her whole head, it just clipped in to the back of her head and made a group of beautiful curls. They are typically quite expensive and he gave it to her as a graduation gift. She was so thankful!

By the time she got home and dressed in her beautiful silver dress, along with her beautiful long curls, she felt like a princess. Jesse allowed her to wear a bit of makeup for this special night; a light pink lipstick and some black mascara. Her grandparents were there waiting, along with her aunt and it was already such a special day.

Mike drove with Hanna in his lavender Chevelle, which he only used on very special occasions. Jesse followed with the truck, so they could bring her motorized wheelchair home at the end of the ceremony. The rest of her family and friends were not far behind. Once again, Hanna felt like a princess. She enjoyed riding alongside her dad who always made her feel special. He was the best date ever!

Once at school, Mike carried Hanna in and up the steps to the stage. A couple of guys had already lifted her heavy motorized wheelchair up there. Once Mike had her situated, he went and found his seat with the rest of her family. Of course, Jesse had to make a quick trip up on stage to straighten her dress and touch up her hair. Then she quickly returned to her seat. All the while, her grandma was taking pictures.

Pomp and Circumstance; the Graduation March,

started playing (Mrs. Jones, the music teacher played the piano) and all of her classmates came walking in, two at a time and when they reached the stage, they would separate, each one of them coming up the stairs on either side of the stage. Then they would walk to their assigned seats. The girls were each dressed so pretty and the boys were very handsome, dressed in a shirt and tie. They all looked very nice and when the music stopped, they all sat down.

A couple of her classmates gave a speech and then some of them, including Hanna, received awards for various things. Hanna received hers for maintaining a straight-A report card for the entire year. After the awards, they finally got to handing out the diplomas.

As each name was called, her classmate would walk up to Mr. Risner, take their diploma and shake hands. When Hanna's name was called, she was able to walk up to Mr. Risner independently, take her diploma, shake his hand and return to her seat under her own power. It was all very exciting!

At the end of the ceremony, Mrs. Jones, once again began playing the music. Each of her classmates exited the same way they had entered, going off each side of the stage and then meeting in the front to walk out. As the last two students were exiting the stage, Mike and his friend hurried and lifted Hanna, wheelchair and all, to the floor, so that she could march out of the gym with her class. Hanna was grinning from ear to ear as she thought to herself, "I am just like everyone else and I am on the top of the world!"

Everyone met out front, congratulating one another and showing off their diplomas. Each of her graduating classmates had their own families and friends there and they were heading off to their own celebrations. Hanna said her goodbyes, knowing that she wouldn't see many of them until the fall when she started high school and others not for a very long time, unless they were neighbors or close friends. She now understood what it meant to be bittersweet.

Hanna had successfully completed her elementary school years, four of which were actually in school with two that didn't require winter tutoring. She had learned through trial and error that she was just like everyone else in many regards, but more importantly, she discovered that **being different is okay**. Everyone is special in some way and that's what makes us who we are. Hanna came to figure out that she didn't want to be like everyone else, but rather, she just wanted to be Hanna.

About the Author

Laurie was born in 1956, diagnosed with muscular dystrophy at the age of two, but eventually getting a correct diagnosis of Spinal Muscular Atrophy Type 2 at the age of 17. She used crutches and braces from the time she was diagnosed until she was five years old and then used a manual wheelchair until the week before her eighth grade graduation. She has used a power wheelchair ever since.

Laurie graduated from high school with honors, attended Arizona State University, where she earned a bachelor's degree in communication disorders and then went on to San Diego State University, earning a Master's degree in rehabilitative counseling. She also holds a clear professional teaching credential for elementary education. Laurie was unable to obtain employment until she was 45 years old, not for lack of qualifications, but solely due to discrimination. Once given the opportunity, her career was on the fast track. She worked for nine months as a program manager for an independent living center, prior to getting promoted to the Executive Director position for three years.

She was then appointed by Gov. Schwarzenegger to a deputy director position with the State Council on Developmental Disabilities for two years and then promoted to chief deputy director for the next three years with the same agency. Due to health complications, she retired from the demands of such a high powered position and has since become an award-winning published author, having written her memoir, "I Can Dance: My Life with a Disability."

Laurie is married and the mother of two adult children with four grandsons. Her 34-year-old son is a construction contractor and her 30-year-old daughter is a sign language interpreter. Two of her grandsons are from her son and the other two are from her daughter. Laurie managed to live her life, give birth, raise her children and become successfully employed, all the while, living with a significant disability.

As her memoir was not appropriate reading for young people, Laurie decided to take her middle school years; fifth through eighth grade and write a somewhat fictional story on her experiences. Laurie addresses going to school for the first time, the understanding and acceptance of her friends and neighbors, some of the challenges and barriers she encounters, bullying and maturity and other things she experiences as she navigates through those particular years of her life.

This is Laurie's story of how she learned "Being Different is Okay!"

Being Different is Okay:

My Disability is Part of Who I Am

Laurie Hoirup

Being Different is Okay:
My Disability is Part of Who I Am

Laurie's Legacy
7410 Alma Vista Way
Sacramento, CA 95831
916-469-7695
Laurie@LauriesLegacy.com

ISBN: 978-1507697498

This story encompasses some of the author's recollections and reflections of childhood, but has been fictionalized with names and details having been changed, while conversations are completely fictional.

Illustrations and Cover Design by Yvette Hall

Printed in US

Contents